Their homecoming had been a disaster

Lee had been swept off her feet by the dashing young Argentinian. Three weeks from the day they met they were man and wife. But the honeymoon didn't last.

The sudden death of Fernando's father meant their swift return to the family ranch. Lee's young husband was faced with a host of unfamiliar responsibilities – which he seemed strangely unwilling to shoulder.

His behavior was a puzzle. Then the sun-drenched pampas yielded up an ugly secret, plunging Lee into a nightmare of hatred and suspicion!

D0831328

Other

MYSTIQUE BOOKS

by LILIANE ROBIN

For a free catalogue listing all available Mystique Books,
send your name and address to:

MYSTIQUE BOOKS,
M.P.O. Box 707, Niagara Falls, N.Y. 14302
In Canada: 649 Ontario St., Stratford, Ontario N5A 6W2

Fury on the Pampas

by LILIANE ROBIN

MYSTIQUE BOOKS

TORONTO · LONDON · NEW YORK

HAMBURG · AMSTERDAM · STOCKHOLM

FURY ON THE PAMPAS/first published July 1980

ISBN 0-373-50086-6

PRINTED IN U.S.A.

Chapter 1

"*Madre de Dios...!*"

Stunned, Fernando Valera crumpled into a black leather armchair, his dark eyes staring blindly at the El Greco print on the hotel room wall. Too numbed even to notice that the telegram had slid from his fingers, he was still slumped there when Lee emerged from the washroom, blotting her lipstick with a tissue.

"All right, darling, I'm ready to go...." Her cheerful voice faltered when she saw her husband's pale complexion and defeated posture. Stepping closer to him uncertainly, she inquired, "Fernando, what's the matter? Aren't you feeling well?"

Slowly he raised his eyes to her concerned face. "I... went down to the desk to see whether there was any mail for us," he replied bleakly. "The clerk gave me this." Locating the telegram beside his left foot, he picked up the slip of paper and handed it to her.

It was from Fernando's teenage sister in Argentina: "Father dead. Return at once. Eviana."

"Oh, my lord," Lee breathed. Shaken, she cast a compassionate glance at her husband, who was still in shock. Lee could think of nothing meaningful to say. Instead she stepped behind Fernando's chair and put a consoling hand on his shoulder.

Half an hour earlier they had checked into this luxury hotel in Madrid, laughing and carefree, on a honeymoon that was turning into a five-week odyssey through Mediterranean Europe. How wrapped up they had been in each other, how unaware of the cruel blow that fate held in store for them!

"What now, Fernando?" she asked softly, breaking the long silence.

He shrugged. "We'll have to go home. We've missed the funeral, of course, but we can't leave Eviana all by herself. I'll make the arrangements...in a minute."

Lee squeezed his shoulder sympathetically.

The wire was dated September 13, four days ago. Eviana had sent it to their hotel in Rome, and it had then followed them to Cannes, St. Tropez, Toledo and finally Madrid. Considering how relaxed the newlyweds had been about sticking to the itinerary Fernando had sent home, it was a wonder the message had reached them at all.

"We'll have to leave as soon as possible," Fernando said abruptly. "I'm going to book us onto the first available flight to Buenos Aires."

Lee said nothing, but her husband must have sensed her disappointment for he turned toward her with an expression that beseeched her understanding. "I'm sorry we have to cut our honeymoon short, my darling."

"It isn't that," she told him softly. "It's . . . my parents were expecting us. . . ."

"I know," he sighed and sank back into the leather armchair. "It's a pity we won't have time to visit Boston, *querida*. I was looking forward to it, also."

Lee gnawed her lower lip pensively. She had been looking forward so much to going home; they had planned a two-week stay in the United States, a last visit before she abandoned her safe, familiar way of life to become the wife, rather than the bride, of a wealthy Argentinian rancher. Lee had also hoped that a face-to-face meeting with her charming husband of five weeks would overcome her parents' reservations about the wedding, which had taken place without them, so hastily and so far from home.

"You do understand, don't you?" Fernando was gazing anxiously into her face.

She mustered an encouraging smile for him. "Of course. I'll just telephone my parents and tell them what's happened," she replied, gesturing in the direction of the antique-style phone on the beach-wood table beside the bed.

Fernando nodded, his features resuming the pained, preoccupied expression he'd been wearing as she entered the room. "All right," he murmured and heaved himself out of the chair. "I'll go settle our hotel bill and make the plane reservations. . . . Please give my apologies to your parents. I wouldn't know what to say to them right now."

"I'm sure they'll understand, darling." The tears in Lee's eyes as she watched him leave were as much for herself as for her bereaved husband.

HER PARENTS HADN'T UNDERSTOOD. As she replaced the gracefully-curved telephone receiver on its cradle, Lee sighed and wondered what it would take to convince them that her marriage hadn't been just a reckless whim. This phone conversation had ended typically, with the cool observation that Lee was obviously old enough to run her own life. After all, she'd made the decision to marry without consulting anyone, hadn't she? No messages of congratulation had been forwarded from the rest of the family, no expressions of love, only a grudging "good luck" amid all the hurt feelings.

Suddenly Lee had the terrifying sensation that she'd been set adrift, that all the threads binding her to her family, friends and home had been severed, leaving her alone on the threshold of a strange new world. Alone? How could she be alone when she had Fernando by her side? Nonetheless, she shivered as she turned away from the telephone.

Ten minutes later Fernando still hadn't returned from his errand. Too restless to wait any longer, Lee scooped up her handbag and went downstairs to find him. The desk clerk directed her to a drawing room off the main lobby, where a tasteful arrangement of chairs, divans and ottomans radiated outward like the spokes of a wheel from a massive iron fireplace set into the long wall opposite the door. In one corner of the love seat nearest to the grate sat Fernando, gazing darkly into the amber depths of a glass of whiskey.

"*There* you are," Lee sighed with relief. "You were gone so long I began to worry."

He turned slowly toward her and blinked hard a

couple of times, and it suddenly dawned on her that the drink in his hand might not be his first. But then he replied, in a taut and perfectly articulate voice, "We're booked on a flight leaving at five-thirty tomorrow morning. And I've taken care of the hotel bill. Did you reach your parents?"

She nodded. "Dad wasn't there, so I spoke to my mother."

"Naturally she was deeply disappointed at our change of plans?"

"Of course. But she'll get over it."

Fernando gazed thoughtfully at her. "And you? Will you get over it?" he asked softly.

Sitting down beside him, Lee reached out and took his free hand. "I'm already over it," she said with a smile. "I'm your wife. Wherever you go, I'll follow. Until death do us part."

For several moments his dark eyes traveled hungrily over her face, taking in the short blond hair, the rosy complexion, the sapphire-colored eyes that one so seldom saw in Latin American countries. This young woman with the supple body and the soft inviting lips, this was his wife. A tragic telegram had dashed the romantic fervor of the five idyllic weeks just past, but Lee was his forever. Squeezing her slender hand, Fernando murmured, "Sometimes I wonder whether I deserve you, Lee."

She started. "Why do you say that?"

Smiling faintly, he replied, "It's just a thought that passes through my head from time to time...."

DINNER WAS A SOMBER MEAL, cut short by the absence of live entertainment and their unspoken agree-

ment to refrain from the sort of lighthearted ban-
ter that had made dining such a pleasure in so many
other cities. It wasn't until they had returned to
their room to pack that Lee realized her husband
hadn't said a single word about his father that
evening. She glanced briefly at Fernando, who was
folding his clothes with rapid motions into a large
leather suitcase. Perhaps it would do him good to
talk about Ramon Valera.

Licking her lips, Lee remarked as casually as she
could, "You've never really told me about your
father, darling. What sort of man was he?"

Fernando looked up sharply before replying, "A
strong man, with a rigid, old-fashioned set of
values. Some people envied him; most liked him.
But everybody who knew him respected him and
even feared him."

"You make him sound larger than life."

"In a way, I suppose he was," Fernando conceded
with a mirthless smile. "Many Argentinian landowners are taking it easy in the cities and letting
their staff look after things for them. My father
always swore that this fashionable idleness was a
betrayal of their heritage. He insisted that the Valeras manage their own property. It takes a big man
to run a ranch like ours," he said pensively. "A
tough man. He was certainly up to it."

"And you're wondering whether you can step
into his shoes," Lee murmured with sudden
comprehension.

Fernando seemed not to hear her. "Father was
always after me to take a more active part in the
management of the *estancia,* but I wouldn't listen to
him. I was only twenty-three. There was plenty of

time to learn about those things," he said ruefully. "Now I'm twenty-four and time has run out."

"But you're your father's son," Lee pointed out encouragingly. "You grew up on that ranch—it's practically in your blood. I'm sure you won't have any trouble—"

Cutting her off with a short, bitter laugh, Fernando said, "Any resemblance between my father and me is purely physical, *querida*. Eviana's the one who should be running that ranch. She inherited his strong will and passionate nature. And last year, after she'd graduated from the convent high school in San Luis and I'd completed four years of university, Eviana was the one who spent all her time poking around the stables and riding inspection with the foremen while I loafed around with my friends and had a good time." Sadly he shook his head.

Lee felt her heart constrict with sympathy for him. Tradition had dictated the role he must play in the family, and she suspected it wouldn't sit well with him at all. It wasn't difficult to guess what Ramon Valera had planned for his daughter—a basic high school education and then marriage to the son of some other wealthy landowner of the region. Her own parents had mapped out much the same sort of future for Lee.

Fernando had resumed packing his clothing, and Lee studied him for a moment before turning her attention back to her own suitcase. Her husband was rather tall, with dark eyes and handsome, regular features. His lean, muscled body was as agile as a panther's. And she had found him capable of both great patience and quiet stubbornness, belying the stereotyped image of the fiery-tempered Latin.

"You know, *querida*," he said now in a muffled voice, "I never truly appreciated how much my father loved me...until today. He sent me to the finest schools, turned a blind eye to all my faults ...." Pausing with both arms braced against his suitcase, Fernando heaved a broken sigh. "When I left Argentina, I never dreamed that he would die before I got back. I only regret that we parted on such unfriendly terms."

Lee raised an eyebrow. "You quarreled?"

"I'm afraid so," he sighed. "I didn't want to go to the ranchers' conference in Paris. We had a terrible argument about that."

"Why didn't you want to go?" Lee asked with a smile. "Besides the fact that you couldn't have foreseen our meeting there."

"I'm not sure myself," Fernando confessed. "Possibly I was rebelling at being ordered to attend. It's all academic now, anyway," he concluded, slamming his suitcase shut.

A moment later Lee closed the second piece of luggage, and while her husband was moving both cases into the closet she began to turn down the bed. "I wouldn't worry too much about your disagreement with your father, darling," she called over her shoulder. "He probably forgot all about it the moment your plane took off from Buenos Aires. Besides, didn't he send us his heartiest congratulations when you wrote and told him we were getting married? And weren't all his letters after that quite warm and affectionate?"

"Yes," Fernando replied hesitantly.

"Then stop tormenting yourself and tell me

instead whether you're sorry you came to Paris,"
Lee demanded mischievously.

By way of reply, he turned her gently around,
cradled her face in his hands and kissed both her
eyelids. "Sorry I met you?" he murmured, enfold-
ing her in a tender embrace that set her heart
racing. "Never, my darling. I feel incredibly blessed
just to know you."

SUNRISE. A GLOWING REBIRTH, easily the most beautiful
moment of the day. Seen from a plane cruising
miles above the earth, daybreak was an awe-
inspiring event. At first the sky surrounded them
like the interior of a royal blue teacup, pouring out
a drop of rosy fire at the edge of the horizon. And
then the flame spread, bathing heaven and earth in
its brilliant glow, chasing blushing clouds out of the
way and revealing an endless expanse of ocean, its
drowsy calm broken here and there by the wake of
a toy-size ship.

"Oh, darling, isn't it breathtaking?" Lee
breathed.

There was no reply from her husband. Turning,
she discovered that he was fast asleep. *Good, let him
rest*, she thought. He'd got little enough sleep the
previous night, upset not only by the death of his
father but also by the thought of the weighty
responsibilities that awaited him as the new *patron* of
the ranch.

Suddenly Lee felt ill. She heard her pulse pounding like an enraged kettle drum in her ears. She felt
quite nauseous and her eyes abruptly refused to
focus. Closing them tightly, she leaned back in her
seat and forced herself to remain absolutely still.

What was the matter with her? She'd never been airsick before. Granted, she had only sipped at her coffee that morning, hardly touching the continental breakfast served by the smartly dressed Iberian Airlines hostess. Or, perhaps, it was the fact that she'd slept so badly the night before that was causing the steel band to tighten around her temples....

"Are you all right, *señora?*"

Opening her eyes Lee saw one of the hostesses bending over her, polite concern on her face.

"No, I'm not," Lee confessed in a half whisper. "I'm dizzy and nauseous."

"It's probably just a touch of airsickness. Shall I get you something for it?"

Lee nodded and the stewardess disappeared toward the tail of the plane, returning a moment later with a plastic cup half-filled with water and a small blue pill.

"What sort of drug is this?" Lee inquired uneasily. She had already had the terrible experience—not on her honeymoon, thank goodness— of taking a patent medicine in a foreign country and discovering that its side effects were worse than the original ailment.

"It's a very gentle sedative for your stomach," the stewardess explained with a smile. Still a little dubious, Lee took the pill and swallowed it with a gulp of the water. Then she handed the cup back to the hostess who assured her, "I'll come back in a few minutes and check on you."

Fernando was still sleeping peacefully beside his wife, undisturbed by the conversation that had gone on around him. As she gazed at his face, free at last of the anxiety Eviana's telegram had etched on it the previous evening, Lee had to repress the impulse to smooth his dark hair with her hand. He looked just like a little boy, dreaming about the presents Santa would bring him in nine weeks' time. Was that the quality that had drawn her to him that first day, when he had accidentally knocked her into the painting she'd been watching a street artist complete in Montmartre? Once Fernando had offered to buy the canvas, the artist had ceased his railing and had turned his attention to the blue and ocher stains on her sleeve, dabbing at them with a pungent chemical he kept in a small bottle in the pocket of his jeans. Fernando had later given her the painting as a souvenir and had invited her to have a strawberry crepe with him. And that was how it had all begun.

Lee was on the last week of a European holiday and should have returned to complete her final undergraduate year at Boston Women's College. But Fernando had persuaded her to stay just another few days, and then another week. She had missed registration day, then the first week of classes. Ignoring her parents' pleas to come home, Lee had let the handsome Argentinian rancher sweep her off her feet. A university degree, she reasoned, could be acquired anytime, but a Fernando Valera rarely entered a woman's life twice. Together they "did" Paris, as the self-possessed American girl fell deeply and hopelessly in love. If only their fling could go on forever!

And then, as a fall of golden leaves on the Champs Elysées heralded the onset of autumn, Fernando had proposed marriage. Lee had felt like Cinderella. Three weeks to the day after their chance meeting in the winding streets of Montmartre, they had become man and wife.

Suddenly the stewardess was bringing lunch trays.

"Lunch?" Lee cried with dismay. "But we just had breakfast."

"You've been sleeping," the hostess told her. "You looked very peaceful and the color was returning to your face, so I decided not to disturb you."

"What? Were you sick, *querida*?" Suddenly Lee realized that Fernando was wide awake beside her.

"Just a touch of airsickness," she replied, feeling a little sheepish. "It's completely gone now. I'm fine."

"You should have wakened me."

"For something as trivial as that, when you were so badly in need of rest?" she said with a smile. "It wasn't necessary."

Neither of them had any appetite for lunch. Fernando waved his tray away, but Lee forced herself to eat the meat and some of the salad. Shortly after the trays had been collected again, Fernando glanced at his watch and announced, "We should be setting down at Rio within the hour."

Rio de Janeiro was the only scheduled stopover on this flight to Buenos Aires. Sure enough, roughly three-quarters of an hour later Lee felt the peculiar near-weightless sensation that signaled they were losing altitude.

At first all she saw was the bay, its islands a huddle of ominous dark shapes like a tribe of giant walrus asleep in the shallows. And then the plane banked, and a shining, white city suddenly came

into view, a Chinese puzzle of tall buildings shelter-
ing astonishing green parks and a sports stadium,
which looked from the air like a huge hubcap fallen
on its side. The captain got on the public address
system and gave several of the dark humps
names—Sugar Loaf, with its warlike cable train
station, and Corcovado, where the famous statue
of Christ spread its arms over the city. It was a
working day, but the beaches were visibly
crowded.

After a brief stop to refuel and take on passengers, they were airborne again, headed south.
Fernando was very quiet. Thoughtful and anxious,
he had to be thinking about his reunion with his
sister and about the house and property for which
he had suddenly become responsible. Lee leaned
back in her seat and recalled the faces in the photo-
graph that her husband had once shown her—a far
more revealing portrait of the Valera family than
Fernando had ever consented to paint for her
verbally.

Ramon Valera, a tall, powerful man in his fifties
with flashing eyes and dynamic features, had been
staring almost belligerently into the camera. Eviana, not yet turned nineteen, had the same dark
eyes and sensual mouth as her older brother, but
her expression was as set and willful as her
father's. A proud and passionate Latin, she was
probably one of those people who either love or
hate on first sight.

Lee wasn't aware she had sighed until Fernando
turned to her and inquired, "What's wrong, *querida*?"

"Tell me about your ranch," she said evasively.

"But I've already told you all there is to tell," her

husband protested. "It's a piece of land located about three hundred miles inland, west of Buenos Aires. We raise horses and grow cereal grains."

"You said it was isolated," Lee persisted. "How isolated?"

Fernando exhaled gustily. "San Luis is the nearest large city, about 125 miles from the house. There's a railway station fifteen miles from the village, but the roads leading to the station are so bad that we don't bother with the train—we drive or ride horseback, depending on the distance to be traveled. Our nearest neighbors—"

"Back up a little," she cut in. "You never mentioned a village before."

"Why should I?" he laughed. "Your interrogation was never this close before. It's not worth talking about, *querida*—just an unimportant cluster of huts that sprang up on the outskirts of the ranch to house the families of our *peons*. It doesn't even have a name."

"And how far is it from the ranch house to this nameless village?" Lee asked, a little more sharply than she'd intended.

The expression of discomfort on Fernando's face gave her a twinge of conscience. "It's a fifteen minute ride on horseback," he finally replied. "And our nearest neighbors are an hour and a half away by automobile."

Lee glanced up suddenly. "But you just said they were only fifteen minutes away," she protested.

"The *peons'* village is fifteen minutes away," he pointed out with a patient smile. "I was talking about the neighboring ranches. There's a considerable difference, *querida*. We value our workers, but we don't fraternize with them. Don't look so dismayed," he laughed. "We have a class system in Argentina. You'll get used to it."

Numbly, Lee nodded, wondering what other ideas and attitudes her husband had been raised with, so many of which were foreign to her.

"Does it bother you that we're going to be so far away from other people?" Fernando asked conversationally.

"N—No. Large cities wear me out. Besides, I'm not going to be all by myself, am I?" Just then their eyes met in a moment of mutual adoration and Lee felt herself melt. She could enjoy purgatory as long as her husband was by her side.

"Well, whenever you feel a craving for traffic jams and department stores, just let me know," Fernando told her. "We can drive into Buenos Aires for a weekend, inhale some pollution, do a little nightclub hopping. . . ." His voice faded slightly on the last word, and he continued in a more subdued tone, "Buenos Aires is quite large and cosmopolitan. I think you'd like it. It might even remind you of the United States. You'll be able to see some of the city when we transfer from Ezeiza Airport to the smaller airfield used by domestic lines." He fell silent then, and Lee watched him quietly, half-afraid to pursue the conversation.

Finally she ventured in a gentle voice, "Isn't there something I can do to help you, darling?"

He shook his head. "I'm afraid not. I have a lot of thinking to do right now. You understand, don't you, *querida*?"

Of course she understood, but it was disappointing nonetheless to have to watch her husband turn inward for strength at a time like this, when she stood ready to support him in his grief. That telegram from Eviana had changed him somehow—he simply wasn't the same man.

Chapter 2

It was four in the afternoon, local time, when the plane touched down at the airport. A light mist had veiled the forest of skyscrapers during their approach, but as the plane had dipped below the clouds Lee had glimpsed enclosed green spaces and the wide network of avenues leading right down to the bank of the broad estuary called Rio de la Plata, "river of silver." This was a huge city, the home of seven million people.

As the minibus carried Fernando, Lee and a small group of quiet travelers the twenty-five miles from the international to the national airport, more of Buenos Aires was revealed: rows of steel-and-glass cubes vying with centuries-old buildings for space along the sides of breathtaking boulevards, streets careening off at right angles from picturesque plazas, leading to housing developments that were springing up over areas measured in tens of square miles.

Suddenly Lee heard Fernando groan beside her. She turned and saw him leafing through a domestic airline schedule.

"Damn!" he muttered. "According to this, there was only one flight to San Luis today, and it took off an hour ago."

"What can we do?" Lee asked.

"Don't worry," he told her, disgruntled at being inconvenienced. "When we get to the airport I'll see if we can charter a plane from one of the small independent companies. Then, before we leave Buenos Aires, I'll telephone Eviana and ask her to send Ricardo to meet us in San Luis with a car."

Ricardo. That would be Ricardo Ruiz. Fernando had mentioned him once or twice in an earlier conversation. Ricardo was the overseer of the agricultural operation of the ranch, one of Ramon Valera's most trusted assistants. Ricardo also had an excellent rapport with the *peons*, or field workers, and knew how to get an honest day's work out of them, Fernando had said. The phrasing of that compliment had set Lee's teeth on edge, for he'd implied that no *peon* would voluntarily earn his pay....

Fernando had no difficulty hiring a plane and pilot to get them to San Luis. Agreeing to meet the twin-engine craft on the parking apron, he strode to the pay phones in the terminal to call the ranch. From what she could hear of the conversation, Lee deduced that Eviana was visiting Ramon's grave, and that Rosa, who had been the Valeras' housekeeper for nearly thirty years, had burst into tears at the sound of Fernando's voice.

NIGHT HAD FALLEN when their small plane touched down on San Luis's well-lighted airfield. The terminal building at Ezeiza had made the one they now entered look makeshift by comparison. Lee couldn't help noticing the heavily marked floor tiles and the well-worn furniture in the spacious waiting room.

Suddenly a man stepped forward and offered his condolences, and Fernando reached out and shook his hand. "Ricardo, it's good to see you again." Then, turning to Lee, he said, "Darling, I've told you about Ricardo Ruiz, haven't I?"

Ricardo looked about thirty. Slightly shorter than Fernando and obviously weathered by the outdoor life he led, he still looked eminently civilized in a short jacket of supple leather and impeccable brown slacks.

"So this is the new *señora*? You've chosen well; she's beautiful." Ruiz's voice was friendly enough, but as Lee's eyes met his light brown ones she thought she glimpsed in them a fleeting annoyance or a flash of disapproval, instantly suppressed. When Lee replied to the introduction in fluent Spanish, she caught another flash of his enigmatic eyes.

Ricardo waved them outside then, to where a station wagon stood parked beside the door. As he saw to the baggage, Fernando assisted Lee into the backseat of the car, then took the passenger's seat in front. At last Ricardo slid behind the wheel, put the wagon in gear and headed west.

They'd been driving in silence for several minutes when Fernando cleared his throat and asked, "Was my father ill?"

"I don't think so, *señor*."

"How did it happen?"

"It was immediately after dinner," Ricardo began

in a flat voice. "Your sister had just gone up to her room and Samantha was serving coffee. Dominic and I were going over the weekly work reports with your father when he suddenly clutched his chest and collapsed. We tried to revive him while Samantha phoned for the doctor, but there was nothing we could do. He was dead. All Dr. Chandler could do when he arrived was confirm that Señor Valera had had a heart attack."

Fernando was silent for several seconds. Then he inquired, "How did Eviana take it?"

"Badly at first. Dominic and Rosa went upstairs to tell her. Apparently she became hysterical. Rosa sat up with her all that night. But by morning she seemed well enough, and she bore up admirably during the funeral...."

It was a bumpy ride over a poorly maintained road, but with apparent lack of concern for both car and passengers, Ricardo kept the accelerator pedal pressed almost to the floor. Bounced and jostled around in the backseat while a nightmarish landscape slid past her window, Lee began to feel nauseous again. It was probably just the result of her fatigue and the tension that had marked the entire day, she thought. She lowered the window beside her and breathed deeply of the warm night air, which helped considerably.

After two hours they reached a tiny village consisting of a small white church surrounded by low cottages. Ricardo turned onto a dirt road, followed it for just over a mile and then swung around a curve. Suddenly a huge house loomed out of the night, blazing with lights and surrounded by outbuildings. This had to be the main ranch house.

The station wagon crossed a tiled courtyard and halted near the front door. As Fernando was helping Lee out of the car, the door flew open and a heavyset woman was silhouetted against the light spilling onto the porch.

"Good evening, Rosa," Fernando called.

"Good evening, *señor*," the servant replied, and stepped aside to let them come inside the house. As she entered the vestibule she notice Rosa's old, lined face, stamped indelibly, it seemed, by sadness. And yet, in spite of the tragic reason for their unexpected arrival, the housekeeper greeted Lee with a smile. "Welcome to Casa Rosada, *señora*. May you be blessed with happiness here."

It was her first real welcome to her new home, and Lee appreciated Rosa's kind words. Ramon Valera's death had pushed the wedding into the background, making all other considerations seem slightly sacriligious.

Just then a slender young woman in a black dress appeared at the foot of the stairs, and Lee recognized Eviana from the picture she had seen. Fernando opened his arms to his sister and she rushed into them, sobbing, "Oh, Fernando! I was afraid you'd never get here.…"

When she had calmed down, he told her gently, "You've been a very brave girl until now. I hope you'll continue to be brave."

Touched, Lee felt tears welling in her own eyes as her young sister-in-law made a visible effort to regain control of herself. Finally, wiping away the trails of moisture on her cheeks, Eviana turned to acknowledge the new arrival.

"This is Lee," Fernando said. "I hope you two will become firm friends."

"How do you do?" Eviana said politely, adding as an afterthought, "Did you have a pleasant trip?"

For a moment Lee stared in shock at the cool, dignified expression on the girl's face. Some confusion might have been excusable, given the circumstances of this first meeting, but Eviana was showing her the face of a stranger who wished to remain that way. Swallowing the consoling words she had been about to pronounce, Lee replied shortly, "Reasonably pleasant, yes."

Ricardo had carried the bags inside. Leaving them in the vestibule, he quietly withdrew.

An instant later, Eviana was smiling winningly at her brother. "I'll bet you're hungry," she said. "Rosa's prepared a snack and a whole urn of coffee. Samantha can serve it."

"Samantha has already gone to bed," Rosa interrupted, "and so has Luisa. I'll serve it myself."

"Perfect," Fernando agreed enthusiastically. "But there's no point in setting the dining room table for us. Why don't you just bring a tray into the living room?" So saying, he took Lee by the arm and ushered her through a set of double doors into a room so richly appointed that for a moment she was speechless.

Fernando had described his home in modest terms, leading her to believe that the comforts she'd grown up with would have to join the other fond memories of her past. He had said nothing about lavish paneling, Peruvian pottery, rosewood furniture or carpeting made of animal skins. As though gathered in by the soft glow of well-placed antique porcelain lamps, a circle of comfortable armchairs formed the focus of the room, and it was to these that Fernando was guiding her when a man suddenly stepped out of the shadows.

"Hello, Dominic," said Fernando, apparently unsurprised. "Lee, this is Dominic Fontanera. I've told you about him."

Told her about him? Yes, he'd mentioned that the foreman in charge of livestock was the only child of two loyal Valera employees who had died in a food poisoning epidemic, that young Dominic had then become the ward and protegé of Ramon Valera, who had overseen his education and had made it possible for him to gain skill and experience at the sort of work the boy loved best, namely the breeding of horses. But Fernando hadn't prepared her to meet someone so untypically tall and rangy, with such pale, hazel eyes and such a ruddy complexion. His jet black hair curled gently onto the nape of his neck, framing a gravely handsome face. Still, there was a grim set to his mouth and a hardness to his features that seemed to give a warning not to get too close to this man of the pampas. Could he really be that cold and insensitive? Perhaps underneath the harshness there was some gentleness....

Wordlessly, Dominic inclined his head toward her as she uttered an automatic acknowledgment of the introduction. Then Lee sat down beside Fernando and Eviana. Dominic remained standing, one elbow propped against the ornate secretary behind her.

Rosa came back with a tray of cups and saucers and a huge pot of coffee, which she served immediately. The fragrant brew was too good to resist, and Lee had emptied her cup before Rosa brought in the second tray, loaded with *platitos*: wedges of meat and fruit on crackers, slices of sausage and miniature doughnuts.

The housekeeper was about to leave the room when Fernando called her back. "Stay for a moment, Rosa. You were there when my father died and I'd like to talk about it one last time."

Until that minute, Fernando had acted as though his absence had been only overnight, as though nothing had happened while he was away. If Lee hadn't witnessed his grief when the telegram had arrived, she might have believed his cold, detached facade. Fernando had evidently decided it would be a waste of energy to make a display of his sorrow, since nothing could bring his father back to life. Lee wasn't sure she agreed.

"Ricardo has told us how quickly it happened," Fernando continued. "Are you sure father didn't complain of any illness just before he died?"

Eviana shook her head.

"We had no warning at all," Dominic stated. "If he'd been in any discomfort I would have known about it, for we had spent most of that afternoon together in the foaling stall helping a mare give birth. Your father appeared to be enjoying his usual good health."

"At lunch all he could talk about was meeting his new daughter-in-law when you returned to the ranch in two weeks. He was very excited about it," Rosa added tearfully.

"It was all over in a matter of seconds," Dominic resumed abruptly. "First thing the following morning I sent word to your cousin, *Señora* Alexia. She and Jorge rushed right over. I notified some of the neighboring ranch owners as well, telling them of plans for the funeral."

Cut completely out of the conversation, Lee felt like a ghost that nobody could see or hear. Why was her husband making no effort to involve her? This was a family tragedy—wasn't she part of it? As her blue eyes traveled in pained confusion from Fernando to Dominic, who was ignoring her, to Eviana, who made no attempt to conceal her indifference toward the interloper, they settled at last on Rosa's round face. Only the housekeeper had shown her any kindness. With a pang of apprehension, Lee wondered whether she would ever really be accepted into her husband's family. Perhaps her parents had been right after all....

Almost as though he'd read her mind, Fernando turned to his wife. "*Querida*, forgive me. I'd forgotten what a long day this has been. All those hours spent traveling must have exhausted you. Rosa, is the *señora's* room ready?"

"*Si, señor*. I've prepared the bedroom adjoining yours, as you requested."

"Good. Why don't you take up the bags? Dominic can help you."

Suddenly launching himself into the circle of light, Dominic crossed the room in several long strides. "It's all right, Rosa. I can take care of them myself," he assured her, casting a dark look at Fernando.

With a murmured good-night, Eviana excused herself and went upstairs to bed. Rosa and the newlyweds followed her up the gleaming sweep of stairs. Halfway down a long corridor the housekeeper opened a door and waved Lee inside.

"It's all right, darling," Fernando told her. "I'm right next door. There's a connecting door between our rooms." Then, with a loving glance that promised a visit through the connecting door that very night, her husband disappeared into his room.

Rosa closed the drapes and withdrew, leaving her new mistress to examine her quarters. It was an elegant, comfortable bedroom with feminine furnishings and accessories, but the many long hours spent getting here, the jet lag and the uncomfortable automobile ride from the San Luis airfield had all taken their toll. As soon as she'd located the bed, oversized and covered with a flowered quilt, Lee collapsed onto it.

She heard Dominic bringing the luggage into Fernando's room next door. Then there was a gentle tap at her own door and the foreman was setting her matching blue cases down beside the vanity table. "Thank you, Dominic," she said, giving him a weary smile.

He said nothing, just nodded his head and left.

"I hope you'll like it here...that you'll love this house as much as I do." Fernando was standing in the doorway that connected their bedrooms as though waiting for an invitation to enter. "I'd also like you and Eviana to get along well," he added with an uncertain smile.

Lee had to smile back. "There's no reason we shouldn't, once she's over the shock of your father's death," she replied, wanting very much to believe that it was shock and grief causing her sister-in-law to behave so coldly toward her. She motioned for her husband to come inside. As he approached the bed, and sat down on its edge she saw that his features were weary and drawn. "Something is bothering you," she said, reaching up and smoothing his furrowed brow with her fingertips. "What is it?"

"Nothing. Why do you ask?"

"You look so worried all the time."

"That's just fatigue. Aren't you tired? I think we should both try to get some sleep." As he got up Fernando assured her, "In a couple of weeks we'll be sharing one large bedroom. I wanted to have renovations done on our quarters, but we'll have to wait a decent length of time before we call in the contractors. You understand, don't you, *querida?*"

"Of course," Lee breathed, drawing him back down for a warm, passionate good-night kiss.

Chapter 3

Lee was awakened the following morning by a ray of warm sunlight that had somehow managed to get past the folds of her drapes. For several seconds after opening her eyes, she was disoriented. Then she remembered where she was and glanced over at the half-open door to Fernando's bedroom. From the silence in the next room Lee gathered that her husband was still sleeping. Quietly she got up, slid her feet into her slippers and opened the drapes.

The countryside, which had been cloaked with darkness the night before, was now basking in the brilliant Argentinian sun, capped by a sky of crystalline blue. Fascinated, Lee opened the window and inhaled the sweetness of springtime. Suddenly she remembered that the seasons were reversed in the southern hemisphere. While North America was sliding dully into winter, the pampas were bursting with new life. Cultivated fields stretched all the way to the horizon, a carpet of various shades of green broken only by a road and several paths. The illusion of a carpet was enhanced by the very flatness of the land. As far as the eye could see, only an occasional clump of bushes or a hedge interrupted the vast sweep of the plain.

At the front of the house, to her extreme left, Lee saw the outer curve of an artistically land-scaped garden overflowing with vibrant red, yellow and purple blossoms. Slightly farther off, also to the left, rose the outbuildings. That morning a groom was currying a magnificent bay stallion in front of the stables, while to the rear stretched several large enclosures, each containing perhaps a dozen horses. To the right of the stables she saw several small houses and one larger one. All looked occupied, and she reasoned that they must be living quarters for some of the staff.

Lee's eyes then moved automatically to the grounds of the main house, which stretched to the right past a huge windmill whose vanes turned lazily in the breeze. The lawns around the *casa* were well-tended and dotted with trees of various ages, some of which had probably been planted by the original Valera family. On the horizon to her right, Lee could make out the steeple of the village church, as well as several of the cottages.

Since marrying Fernando, she had read as much as she could about Argentina, in an attempt to become better acquainted with the country where she and her husband were going to live. But the descriptive phrases in her geography books had come nowhere near capturing the richness of the pampas. Nor had she discovered at Casa Rosada the sophisticated, artificial surroundings described in tourists' brochures. There were no acres of tended lawn or kidney-shaped swimming pools here!

The Casa Rosada, which translated into English as "pink house," was an old family dwelling made of stone. Its exterior bore the patina of age, and its facade had been painted the dusty rose color that had given it its name. Although Lee hadn't had a chance to examine every room in the house, the three she had been in had impressed her with their comfort and their understated elegance.

Daydreaming, she let her gaze wander to the farthest horizon of the Valeras' property, then the clip-clop of hooves brought her abruptly back to reality. A gray stallion was being saddled in front of the stables. Just as she was wondering who was going to ride it, a tall man rounded the corner of the building, moving with the lithe grace of a jungle cat. Lee watched in fascination as he swung himself effortlessly into the saddle. Then, unexpectedly, he turned and looked directly at her. It was Dominic Fontanera.

Lee felt herself shrink involuntarily from the steady appraisal of that flinty gaze. It took an effort of will not to withdraw from the window as he trotted past, never taking his eyes off her face. The night before, she had wondered idly what lay behind his mask, now she wasn't sure she wanted to know. All at once Dominic touched his spurs to the stallion's flanks and they galloped off to the east.

Lee felt inexplicably restless once he had gone. She had a sudden urge to get out of the house and visit the ranch. Wandering into Fernando's room, she was surprised to find it empty; he obviously had risen and left quietly while she was still asleep. A glance at the clock on her dresser gave her the answer—it was already eight o'clock. Hurriedly she washed, dressed and headed downstairs. As she reached the bottom step she heard the muffled sound of angry voices. One of them was Fernando's.

Without being able to make out a word of the argument, which was spoken in rapid patois, Lee followed the sound to a half-open door. Silence fell as she stepped into the dining room. A cursory look around revealed gleaming floor tiles, massive walnut furniture and huge curving bay windows opening onto the spacious yard behind the house. But Lee's attention was centered mainly on her husband, who was standing in the middle of the room and frowning at a young brunette woman setting table for breakfast. The moment he saw Lee in the doorway, he smiled and came over to greet her, at which point the woman recommenced her work with an angry clatter of dishes and silverware.

"Up already?" Fernando asked. "I hope you slept well, *querida.*"

It seemed to Lee that the racket in the dining room grew louder as her husband addressed her.

"Very well, thanks." Lee said, raising her voice to be heard over the din. She stared questioningly at the dark-haired girl.

"This is Samantha," Fernando explained, "Officially she's our linen maid, but she sometimes helps Rosa out when Luisa is ailing."

Samantha turned slowly to face them, revealing a heavy mass of dark hair, a narrow face and shining dark eyes, deep and impenetrable. Lee couldn't help thinking that although she wasn't a classic beauty, Samantha was striking and would be unde-

niably attractive to men. Her sensuous, well-
curved body strained at the fabric of her thin
cotton dress each time she moved. Lee imagined
she had an army of admirers, both on the ranch and
in the village.

Meanwhile Samantha was sizing her up as well,
boldly and almost resentfully, and Lee couldn't help
drawing a comparison between this welcome and
the one she'd received from Eviana and Dominic.
As soon as the maid had left the room, Lee turned
to her husband and remarked with some concern,
"Your people have given me quite a cold reception
so far, Fernando. They make me feel as though
I'm...an intruder...."

Fernando shrugged with annoyance. "You
shouldn't believe that, Lee. If Dominic and the others have seemed aloof, it's because, like Eviana,
they still haven't recovered completely from the
shock of losing my father. You must—"

"Good morning, everybody," Eviana interrupted
in an almost cheerful voice as she strode into the
room. Her hair made a dark frame for her pale face
and she looked very tiny and fragile in her mourning clothes. If she had overheard Lee's complaint
she made no mention of it. But she did seem a little
more cordial than the evening before, even smiling
as she asked Lee, "Did you sleep well?"

"Yes," Lee replied a little warily. "The house is
remarkably quiet."

Just then Rosa came in with a heavily loaded tray,
and soon the room was filled with the aroma of
coffee and the warmth of grilled ham and toast.

Eviana looked surprised to see the older woman.
"Where's Samantha this morning?" she asked.

Rosa shrugged. "Samantha has been moody lately. She stormed into the kitchen just now, complaining that she had enough to do looking after the linen without taking on somebody else's job, as well. I imagine she's gone home."

"What nerve!" Eviana fumed. "She wouldn't have dared to talk that way if father were still alive!"

"Then let her stick to her linens from now on," Fernando cut in sharply. "She's not indispensable, after all. If there's too much work for Luisa to do, then hire another girl."

Rosa frowned.

"I don't think it's a good idea to give in to Samantha," Eviana protested. "You've barely taken your place as head of the household. If the staff were to get the idea that you were weak, it could lower morale around the ranch."

Lee was astonished to hear a teenager, even one as self-possessed as her sister-in-law, talking with such authority about household staff and morale. Meanwhile, Rosa said, "Luisa will be sufficient, *señor*. I only need one helper for the everyday chores, and I can hire a charwoman by the day when there's heavy work to do."

Fernando raised no objection to this and, after a pause to gauge his reaction, Rosa returned to the kitchen. Lee noted that he hadn't responded to his sister's remarks either, and that Eviana had decided not to press the issue. The matter was obviously closed. No further mention was made of the linen maid and her moods, but Lee couldn't help wondering whether the angry discussion she had overheard in the dining room had had anything to do with Samantha's fit of pique that particular morning.

After a fairly lengthy silence, Eviana asked her brother pointedly, "How do you intend to run the ranch?"

"I don't." he replied shortly. "I'm aware of my responsibilities as your legal guardian for the next couple of years and as head of the household and the ranch, but I couldn't possibly step into father's shoes right now. I haven't got the experience to do as effective a job as he did running this place. Therefore I've decided to let Dominic and Ricardo do the work, since they're both so competent. I know I can trust them, just as father did. And I'll have an accountant come out and do our books once a month. That way everything should continue to operate smoothly."

Obviously Fernando had given considerable thought to the handling of the situation. But Eviana had other things on her mind. "You mean you're just going to be a figurehead?" she demanded incredulously. "Father always took care of his own business, and I'm sure he never intended you to—"

"I'll begin my apprenticeship by watching the experts at work, if you don't mind," Fernando interrupted. "Then, when I'm able, I'll take the reins in my own hands."

This reply effectively silenced his sister, and to change the subject Eviana turned to Lee and asked, "How long had you been living in Paris when you and Fernando met?"

Lee gulped hard. She'd been trying to ignore the thick layer of cream in the silver creamer on the table in front of her. Never very fond of cream, she could feel her stomach heave a little at the very sight of it. "Only a couple of months," she replied, forcing herself to smile. "I was on vacation. My home is—was—Boston. That's where we've been the past six years, anyway. I was an army brat until my father retired and took a civilian job. We've lived in Germany, Belgium, England, Spain...."

"Spain? That explains why your Spanish is so good," Eviana remarked.

"You're being very charitable," Lee protested. "My Spanish is far from perfect."

Smiling faintly, Eviana assured her, "I think your accent is charming."

Lee sensed that politeness rather than warmth had motivated the compliment, but decided to acknowledge it anyway. "Thank you, Eviana, what a kind thing to say."

Lowering her eyes to the rim of her coffee cup, Eviana continued, "Aren't you afraid you'll be bored here after the excitement of Boston and Europe?"

"No. I'm not really a city girl at heart. I've always preferred quiet places, far from the crowds and the traffic. Besides, why should I be bored as long as I'm living with the man I love?" Lee rejoined.

Fernando smiled broadly at her. "You're the soul of logic, *querida*."

Eviana let the matter drop. Any conversation that was attempted subsequently fell flat. Toward the end of the meal, Eviana asked suddenly, "Are we going to visit the cemetery this morning?" The question was clearly addressed to her brother, rather than Lee.

"Of course. We can leave right away, if you like," Fernando replied, and Lee immediately chimed in, "I'd like to go, too, and pay my respects, as the newest member of the family."

"I was just about to invite you, *querida*," he said warmly.

Eviana didn't say a word.

THAT AFTERNOON FERNANDO took Lee on a tour of the ranch. Casa Rosada was comprised of much, much more than the lovely old home with its wrought-iron balconies and large flower gardens. It consisted of all the buildings that stood on Valera property: the tool sheds and storage cellars, the stud farm, the rows of shacks that housed some of the field hands and grooms and their families. Casa Rosada was an immense farming establishment, its thousands of acres being brought to life by the Argentinian spring. Farther to the south the land reverted to pampa, with its vast herds of cattle and its famed *gauchos*.

The feather in Ramon Valera's cap, however, had always been the stud farm. Producing a graceful, hardy breed of horses that were valued for many miles around, the breeding operation had made the man's reputation.

The estate had the dimensions of a kingdom. But this vast, prospering freehold, which he had just inherited, seemed to impress Fernando not at all. Lee, on the other hand, was overwhelmed by it. She had known Fernando's family was wealthy and powerful, but somehow that concept had always seemed far removed from the handsome, fun-loving man she'd married. Lee had never seen Fernando in the context of his background, and their extended honeymoon had postponed the moment when image met reality.

Lee's family had never been rich. With regular income from investments her father had made early in his career the Carlisles had been comfortable enough, but they had never had real material power such as Fernando now held in his hands. Never having lacked anything that she wanted, Lee had always thought she was indifferent to wealth...until now. As she gazed at the endless expanse of cultivated land and the outbuildings, which were numerous enough to make a small town, she realized for the first time just how affluent the Valeras were.

"It's hard to believe that all this belongs to you," she whispered in awe.

"It's half Eviana's, don't forget. And there are many properties in the district that are larger and more prosperous than Casa Rosada. Earlier it was divided between my father and his brother, just as I'll divide it between Eviana and myself when the time comes. If you like, we can take a drive around the perimeter of the ranch tomorrow."

Suddenly Lee felt a flush of anxiety. "You could have married any one of the daughters of those other landowners, couldn't you?"

"Possibly," Fernando shrugged. "I never tried."

"And your father blessed our marriage, even though he'd never met me and knew I didn't come from a wealthy family...?"

"Because he wanted me to be happy," her husband concluded with a firmness that dispelled her worry.

But a moment later his face suddenly darkened. Lee slid her hand into his and squeezed it comfortingly. "It's too late for second thoughts, *señor*," she joked. "We're married, for better or for worse, until death us do part."

Shaking himself, Fernando sighed and asked her forgiveness for the fact that he had let his mind wander. "I was thinking that if we'd only come home two weeks earlier...." Then, as though to escape from his regret, he began running toward the stable, pulling Lee behind him. "Come on, we'll visit Carioca," he called over his shoulder.

"Carioca?" she echoed.

"My horse. It's going to be good to see him again."

The interior of the stable was quite dim after the bright sunlight outside. Lee could just make out the row of stalls against one wall, and by straining to discern movement in the semidarkness, she could finally tell which ones were occupied. The air was slightly damp, sweet with the smell of hay and and pungent with the unmistakable but not altogether unpleasant aroma of horses and manure.

"There he is," Fernando said happily, and walked down the row of stalls toward a sleek brown head with a white blaze on its forehead. In spite of the time that had elapsed, Carioca recognized his master. Whickering excitedly, the horse bobbed his head up and down a few times, then thrust a questing muzzle at each of Fernando's pockets in turn. "Looking for a treat, are you?" Fernando asked wryly, then began to stroke the stallion's neck. "Not today, I'm afraid."

"I had to ride him several miles each day while you were gone."

Lee started violently at the sound of Dominic's voice and whirled around. Dressed in a dark shirt and blue denim pants, the foreman was standing against the far wall of the stable, checking some tack.

"If I hadn't ridden him," Dominic continued, striding toward them, "he would have kicked down his stall. He's a spirited beast. Here, let's give him some air."

Carioca whinnied with pleasure as Dominic led him out of his stall and into the yard. As the sun struck reddish sparks from the stallion's generous mane, Lee could appreciate what a beautiful creature he was, with his sleek brown coat and powerful body, every movement of which was accompanied by a rippling of muscles just beneath the skin. Carioca was nervous, too, and pranced like a thoroughbred. She imagined it would take a masterful rider to control him. And Dominic had ridden him every day for two months.

Lee stole a glance at the foreman, feeling again the curious fascination that his taciturnity and his inscrutable hazel eyes had aroused in her the night before. Suddenly she realized that Dominic was gazing at *her*, in the same frank, appraising way as he had done that morning. From close up, however, the effect was quite different. Lee found herself staring helplessly into his sunburned face, unable to tear her eyes away from a look whose still depths made her knees feel weak.

"Have you come to choose a mount for yourself, *señora*?" Dominic finally asked.

Blushing fiercely, Lee replied, "No. I'm afraid I don't know how to ride."

Dominic said nothing, only raised one eyebrow

before remarking casually, "If you'll excuse me, *señor, señora,* I have to check on the corrals." Silently as a shadow, he disappeared.

After a moment Fernando sighed. "The horse is an important mode of transportation in this part of the country, *querida.* Everybody knows how to ride, even the littlest ones. You're going to have to learn—otherwise you'll feel like an outsider."

"Of course, you're right," Lee replied curtly, stung by this thoughtless reminder of her status. "Later, perhaps...."

"There's no hurry, my darling," he said, and smiled indulgently. "Until you're ready to gallop over the pampas with me you can use my car or else one of the pickup trucks belonging to the ranch to get around."

"I must admit, I would feel more confident with a steed that had a steering wheel and a transmission."

Just then Carioca pawed the ground with an impatient hoof. "Sorry, boy, not today," Fernando told him in a soothing voice as he led the snorting stallion back to his stall. "We'll go out for a ride tomorrow morning."

Toward the end of the afternoon, Rosa sent Luisa up to help Lee unpack her bags. It was a beginning. Lee wouldn't truly be moved in until her trunks, containing the rest of her belongings, had arrived from Boston.

She liked Luisa at first sight. Thin and sallow skinned, Rosa's youngest niece wasn't very pretty, but she had an open, honest face and such a pleasant attitude toward life that Lee couldn't help feeling drawn to her.

Once the unpacking was done, Lee sent Luisa back downstairs and sat down to scribble a short letter to her parents, letting them know that she'd arrived safely at the Casa Rosada and giving them her first impressions of the place. Then it was time to dress for dinner.

Fernando had carefully prepared her for this first evening meal, explaining, "Dominic and Ricardo usually join the family for dinner, so don't be surprised to see them at the table. My father began the practice in order to force-feed some business sense into his children. Dinner became a business meeting, where father discussed the running of the ranch with his two trusted foremen. Now it's a tradition, and I have no intention of breaking it."

"A rather unorthodox tradition, isn't it?" Lee had inquired.

"Yes. It shocked and angered many of father's acquaintances, but he ignored their criticism. He saw nothing wrong with sharing his evening meal with his two most devoted employees."

The meal took place in almost complete silence. Visibly self-conscious about assuming the leadership of the household, Fernando remained quiet, and everybody else followed suit. It wasn't the absence of polite conversation that bothered Lee, however; what disturbed her was the empty chair that had been set between Eviana and her brother, and the longing way Eviana kept turning to look at it.

Chapter 4

Early the following morning, in spite of his obvious efforts not to disturb her, Lee heard Fernando getting dressed in the next room. Frowning with curiosity, she slid out of bed and opened the connecting door.

"*Querida*, you're awake!" he said apologetically. "Did I make too much noise? I'm sorry."

He was in dark blue trousers and riding boots, his hands still busy with the tortoiseshell buttons of his leather vest as he came toward her.

"Where are you going?" she asked.

"Before I went to Europe I always used to take Carioca for an early-morning gallop. I've decided to start doing that again," he explained, and as she nodded slowly he added, "When you've learned how to ride you can come with me."

Lee smiled faintly. "Somehow I don't think that'll happen overnight."

"It's up to you, *querida*. You can become a horsewoman slowly or quickly, whichever you want."

"We'll see," she replied thoughtfully. "I've got so

much to get used to first...a whole new way of life...." Lee refrained from telling her husband that she had been feeling rundown lately, attributing her lassitude to the change of climate and perhaps, the food.

"Never mind, take as long as you like, darling. I know how I always used to resent being pushed to learn things right away. Why don't you come out later and meet me on my way back? I'll be coming along the west road about nine o'clock. We can double up on Carioca for the quarter mile or so back to the stable. Then we'll go for that ride I promised you, around the perimeter of the ranch."

He was smiling expectantly at her, so Lee said the only thing she could: "Sure. That sounds like a great idea."

But later on, as Lee lay in her bed listening to Carioca's hoofbeats recede into the distance, she suddenly felt alone and discouraged. The honeymoon was over. Fernando had stepped back into his old ways, leaving her to face this new day in the silent old house without him. From now on she would have to share her husband with everyone else on the ranch and, ultimately, with the ranch itself. Nothing would ever be the same between them again.

Slowly Lee got out of bed and parted the curtains to let in a flood of sunlight. The morning was too beautiful to waste in depressing thoughts. By the time she was washed and dressed, she was humming to herself.

In the dining room, she found that only one place had been set for breakfast—her own. As she pulled back her chair to sit down, Luisa poked her head around the kitchen door and called out, "*Momentito, señora!* I'll be right there." A minute later the girl was serving her a sumptuous breakfast of eggs and sausages and steaming black coffee.

"Where is Eviana this morning?" Lee inquired.

"The *señorita* has gone riding with her brother, *señora*," came the respectful answer.

"Oh. Did they always use to ride together?"

"Before the *señor* left for Europe, you mean? No, *señora*. They hardly ever went out together."

Puzzled, Lee fell silent, and Luisa returned to the kitchen.

Perhaps this shared activity was necessary to help them resolve their grief, Lee reasoned— brother and sister going off alone together to mourn their father. In that case, shouldn't she leave them to their communion? Should she go out to meet her husband or not? Finally she decided to let him finish his ride with his sister in peace.

Once breakfast was over, however, Lee found herself at loose ends. Rather than wander aimlessly around the house, she stepped out the front door into the garden. The sun, though only partway up the morning sky, was already hot, and its light made the brightly colored flowers dazzling. Surrounded by the flowers and the luxuriant greenery of the lawns, Lee could almost imagine herself in an oasis.

All at once she heard shouting from the direction of the stable and decided to investigate. Earlier she had noticed a smaller enclosure just off one of the main corrals and had idly speculated as to its use. This morning she was about to find out, for that was the source of the excitement. A young groom was in the enclosure with an unbroken filly, holding onto her lead line with one hand and waving a leather bit at her with the other. The filly obviously wanted no part of the contraption he was offering and was putting up quite a struggle. Meanwhile, Dominic was leaning on the fence calling advice to his protegé. "Not so rough with her, or she'll kick a hole in your chest!"

Lee looked around. The commotion had brought her all the way from the garden, and she had expected others to come running, as well. But then she realized that on a stud farm this sort of scene was probably commonplace. With a sigh she rested her weight against the wooden enclosure, only a couple of yards from Dominic. Sparing her only a brief nod of acknowledgment, he continued to holler instructions at the groom. "All right, let her go now and close the fence after her."

The young groom slipped the halter off her muzzle and she was off like a shot, her mane flying in the wind as she thundered through the gate into the largest of the corrals, where she performed a series of graceful leaps and bounds.

"She's beautiful," Lee remarked quietly.

"Yes, but she's too nervous and I don't like her temperament," Dominic informed her. "I doubt that we'll keep her."

Lee's jaw dropped in astonishment. The foreman had addressed her in perfect English, with just a trace of an accent.

His lips quirking with suppressed amusement, he added, "I guess the *señor* didn't tell you about me."

"He—he told me you were orphaned and raised

by Señor Valera, but that was all," she stammered, the English words feeling strange to her tongue after speaking nothing but Spanish for two days.

"My father was from San Francisco."

"What? Then you're American!" she declared.

"Only if I renounce my Argentinian citizenship, and I have no intention of turning my back on my mother's native land."

"Have you ever visited the United States?"

He shrugged. "No, never."

"Are you going to someday?" she persisted.

"It's unlikely," came the reply, in a flat voice that seemed to close the subject.

"I'm impressed with your command of the English language," she went on trying a different tack. "Particularly if you've never lived in an Englishspeaking country."

To her amazement, he smiled. "Thank you, *señora*. My father was an excellent teacher."

"But you can't have much occasion to use English around here. How have you managed to keep it up?"

"My father saw to it that I was functionally bilingual," he explained, turning and beginning to stroll toward the stable. "When *Señor* Valera took me in he must have realized how valuable an English-speaking employee would be. He sent me to school, where I could continue to study the language. Your husband and his sister also took courses in English at school, and from time to time we converse." His features had resumed their earlier lack of expression.

"I wonder why your father left San Francisco," Lee murmured, almost to herself.

"Perhaps he wanted to get rich." The voice went flat, effectively cutting off further conversation. Suddenly Dominic turned and called out in Spanish to a passing stable hand, "Go saddle my horse, José. I have an errand to run in the village."

Lee let her gaze wander over the enclosure where the filly was now trotting calmly, avoiding the company of the other horses. "Dominic, if I were to decide to learn to ride, which horse would you recommend for me?" she asked suddenly.

Unhesitatingly he replied, "The black mare with the star on her forehead."

"Why that one?"

"Because she's gentle and obedient, a perfect mount for an inexperienced rider. If you're thinking seriously of taking lessons, why not begin today?" he suggested.

But she shook her head. "No, I'd prefer to wait a few days more...."

Just then the whickering of a horse nearby drew their attention. José had brought the gray stallion into the yard and an old man was helping to tighten the saddle. Lee had to admire the animal, standing there so proudly while the two grooms busied themselves with girth straps and stirrups.

"He's magnificent," she remarked.

"Señor Valera gave him to me two years ago." Had Lee been imagining it or had there been a trace of huskiness to his voice?

"He really loved you, didn't he?" she asked simply.

"As much as I loved and respected him. If he hadn't taken me in and seen to my education I might have wound up digging ditches or cleaning out stables. But he saw things in me, the same things I wanted for myself. He gave me the opportunity to perfect my English and then made it possible for me to become his foreman. I owe everything to him." The frightening intensity of his voice was matched by the fierce gleam in his eyes, and Lee felt vaguely as though he were warning her against some course of action that hadn't even crossed her mind.

Excited at the prospect of a hard run, the stallion was shaking his mane as the old man handed the reins to Dominic. "He's ready to go, *patron*." Then, avoiding any eye contact with Lee, he turned and disappeared. Intrigued by the man's clothes, which were cleaner and better fitting than the outfits worn by most of the men who came and went around the stables, Lee asked Dominic, "Who was that old man?"

"Julian Cartes, Samantha's father. He's my assistant. He's self-taught, but nobody knows horses better than Julian, or can bring a mare through a difficult foaling more competently. Besides his long years of experience, he has an unerring instinct for breeding. And now, if you'll excuse me, *señora*, I have to ride into the village to pick up some medication for one of our colts."

He swung himself in one effortless motion into the saddle and galloped off, raising a cloud of golden dust in his wake. Lee stood motionless, watching him go. He'd given her several privileged glimpses behind his mask that morning. Now, if only she knew how to interpret what she had seen....

"ARE YOU ANGRY WITH ME for tagging along?" Eviana was sitting on a knoll, her legs stretched out in front of her. The coolness of the morning had brought a rosy glow to her cheeks and she seemed much more relaxed than she had the night before. Fernando looked down at her, noting the black silk scarf knotted at her throat and tucked into a gray jacket, and the black trousers that she'd resurrected from a trunk in the basement of the *casa*. Then, with a sigh, he sank down beside her on the sparse grass and shook his head.

"No, I'm not angry. I'm glad to be here with you, glad to be doing the things I've always done in familiar surroundings. I really missed this country while I was away. You know, nowhere in Europe could I find the peaceful openness of our pampas."

"So instead you found a wife."

Fernando gazed thoughtfully at his sister. "What do you think of Lee?" he asked.

Chewing on a blade of grass Eviana replied slowly, "She's very beautiful."

"Is that all? I want to know how you feel about her. Do you like her?"

Eviana looked away. "I'm still too upset by father's death to be thinking of much else...."

"I hope that with time you two will become friends."

She shrugged. "Sure, why not?" she said without conviction, continuing to stare into the distance. Then, before Fernando could pursue the matter, she suddenly asked, "Why did you marry in such a hurry, 'Nando?"

"Love at first sight, I guess," he replied. "Why?"

"Then I was wrong. I thought you married just to please father."

Fernando scowled. "What made you think that?" he demanded.

"Well, wasn't it one of his fondest desires to see you come back with a bride on your arm?" she rejoined, a challenge in her voice.

"I don't see what you're getting at."

This time she turned and stared directly into his face, her lips quirking in a smile. "Come on, Fernando, I'm not a child anymore. I know why father insisted that you represent him at that conference, and it wasn't anything to do with horse breeding. He just wanted to get you away from—"

"That's enough!" he cut her off abruptly.

"There's no need to get all upset. If I've touched a nerve, I'm sorry. I didn't mean to."

"All right," he said, in a calmer voice. "Just let's not talk about it anymore. It's time we got back anyway."

The ride back to the *casa* was a direct contrast to the joyous way they'd galloped away from it two hours earlier. Then they had given their horses their heads and had thundered along a road that had quickly turned into a dirt path between fields of wheat and corn. They had reveled in the sensation of freedom that such a mad dash cross-country had always given them, for brother and sister were both excellent riders. Now, however, as they walked sedately back to the house, Fernando was still frowning and Eviana searched her mind for a way to lighten his mood.

"Shall I bring you up to date on all the exciting things that you missed while you were away?" she suggested at last.

"I'm listening," he said in a disgruntled voice.

"Well, Joachim Primera has left to spend a year on a cattle ranch in the United States. It was his father's suggestion."

"That isn't much of a loss," he remarked dryly.

"His sister joined the convent of the order of the Annunciades at San Rosario one week ago," Eviana went on.

Fernando snorted. "A girl that ugly has no other choice, no matter how rich her father is."

"There's going to be a wedding," she cut him off determinedly. "My friend Carmela Mendoza is marrying the son of a banker in San Luis. I've been invited, but because we're in mourning I would only go for the ceremony. Is that all right?"

Fernando shrugged. "I see no reason why you can't attend a religious service and wish your old school friend luck."

"Good. Ricardo could drive me there in one of the cars," she suggested hopefully.

"All right. Was there anything else?"

"Yes!" she cried, her face lighting up with joy. "Our cousin Alexia has a new baby girl. I saw her last month. What an adorable child! She's so bright and friendly...."

"What are they calling this little prodigy?" Fernando asked.

"Mariana. We really ought to go visit her one day soon. And then you could thank Alexia for rushing over and taking care of everything when father died."

Fernando made a face. "I'd rather write her a letter. All new babies look the same to me."

"Then you don't have to worry, because little Mariana isn't a newborn anymore," Eviana pointed out mischievously. "She's more than two months old."

"I see you're as crazy about children as ever," Fernando observed wryly.

"I certainly am. When I'm married I intend to have dozens of them."

Fernando couldn't help smiling at the thought, and Eviana smiled back at him, glad that she'd been able to erase the frown from his forehead.

"Father wrote to tell you that we had a new *padre* at the church, didn't he?" she continued. Her brother nodded. "He was a great comfort to us when father died. We'll have to thank him, too."

"Can we quicken the pace a little?" he asked abruptly. "I promised Lee I'd take her around the ranch this morning."

"In that case, why don't we cut through the village?" Eviana suggested.

The fretwork steeple of the little church was in sight when Fernando inquired, "And what about Dr. Chandler?"

Eviana shrugged. "He hardly ever changes."

"Did he come to look after father as soon as he was called?"

"Yes," she sighed, "but it was already too late."

They both fell silent after that, thinking about Ramon Valera. In the village they noticed a young man whispering into the ear of a laughing woman with a mass of brown hair, who was carrying a laundry basket on her hip. As the riders drew near, the young man looked up, startled, then disappeared down a lane between two cottages. But the woman glared haughtily at them as they rode past.

Eviana was beside herself. "Did you see that?"

she cried as soon as they were out of earshot. "She didn't even say good morning! The nerve of that woman! I tell you, 'Nando, Samantha gets more insolent every day. You'd think she was proud of the immoral life she leads!"

"What do you know about her life?" he objected. "The juicy tidbits passed around the village by a few gossip mongers can hardly be considered proof of 'an immoral life'."

"I'm not making it up!" Eviana declared hotly. "She just gave us a sample of her arrogance. And as for the rest, goodness knows she makes no secret of it...."

Fernando refused to rise to the bait, he just let his sister chatter on indignantly until her diatribe was finished. By then they were in sight of Casa Rosada.

Lee was waiting for her husband in the yard beside the tack shed, while, not far from the garages, Ricardo was tinkering with the engine of a Land Rover. They were the only two people in sight.

"I want to talk to Ricardo," Eviana told her brother. "Tell Lee I'll see her at lunch." So saying, she rode quickly across the yard, dismounted a few yards from the car and walked over with studied casualness. "Hello, Ricardo. Did the engine break down?"

"It's nothing serious," he replied without raising his head. "Just a dirty spark plug."

"Well, my brother agrees with me," she announced without preamble. "You're going to drive me to Carmen Mendoza's wedding."

He grunted with surprise, but still refused to look at her. "If I have the time."

"You know, any other employer would fire you for taking such a cavalier tone," she pointed out archly.

"That's because I wouldn't have known any other employer since she was a flat-chested kid," Ricardo replied gruffly. His voice sounded slightly hollow as it reverberated inside the Land Rover's engine compartment.

"And do you still think of me as a flat-chested kid?" Eviana demanded.

"No. But I'll always think of you as Ramon Valera's daughter." At last he stood up straight and closed the hood.

"You're going to make the time to drive me to San Luis. You're not indispensable around here, you know," she teased. "I'm sure that you could go away for a few hours and come back to find the ranch running just as smoothly as when you left it."

"Nothing on this earth is irreplacable," he agreed. "But do I really have to drive you to San Luis?"

"Do you hate the prospect that much?"

"That isn't the problem, Eviana." He tried to open the door of the Land Rover, but she planted herself in front of him, her hands on her hips and her dark eyes trained unwaveringly on his face.

"Oh, yes it is," she rejoined. "Look at me, Ricardo. Take a good long look and then tell me honestly—do you find me repulsive?"

"Again?" he sighed. "Eviana, even if I gave you the answer you obviously want to hear, where would that lead us? There can't be anything between us, you know that. You're still a kid."

"So there's twelve years' difference in our ages— so what?" she flared defiantly. "I don't give a damn about that or about what people might think or say about us! I'm going to live my life the way I please and to hell with the rest of the world!"

"Your father wouldn't have liked to hear you talk that way, Eviana," Ricardo said sadly.

"You're right," she admitted with a sigh. "Father was the only person in the world who could have come between us. If he had demanded my obedience he would probably have had it. But he's dead now and there's no one else who can stop be from doing as I like."

Ricardo shrugged. "There's your brother. And you're still below the age of consent, Eviana. He'd never agree to give your hand in marriage to a ranch hand. It'll take years before the social attitudes in the pampas are brought up to date with the rest of the world. You're a full-blooded member of a rural aristocracy. Girls like you simply don't marry men like me," he concluded, his voice tinged with bitterness.

"Then we'll wait until I'm twenty-one," she declared, "Although that might not be necessary."

Shaking his head, Ricardo reached past her and opened the Land Rover's door. Eviana automatically stepped aside and he got behind the wheel. As he turned the key in the ignition, bringing the engine roaring to life, she reached both hands impulsively through the open window, captured his face and planted a lingering kiss on his lips. He didn't fight very hard to get free. Once she'd withdrawn, however, he scolded her, "That was careless. Someone might have seen us."

"So what!"

"You're just a kid," he repeated somberly. "A kid playing with fire. It may seem glorious and romantic now, but wait until next month or next year, when you meet a rich, handsome man from your own social class. Then you'll feel ashamed of yourself for this little fling."

Shaking her head with childish energy, Eviana declared fiercely, "No, Ricardo! I'll never change!"

He smiled sardonically at her from the cab of the Land Rover. "Never say never, Eviana. Only time knows what's in store for us poor mortals." Then he pressed down on the accelerator and the vehicle took off in a cloud of dust, leaving Eviana glaring frustratedly after him.

Chapter 5

Over the course of the next week, life slowly returned to normal at the Casa Rosada. The death of Ramon Valera and the arrival of his new, young daughter-in-law seemed not to have changed things appreciably.

Wracked by spells of malaise, which disappeared as quickly as they came, Lee found it difficult to muster much enthusiasm for anything. She didn't go out very often and, inevitably, the horseback riding lessons had to be put off. Fernando, meanwhile, fell easily into his old habit of going out for long, early-morning gallops, usually alone but sometimes with his sister. On his return to the ranch he would linger at the corrals, or in Dominic's office when the foreman needed his approval or his signature for a business transaction. Although Fernando showed some interest in the stud farm, he seemed totally indifferent to the agricultural side of the operation. His attitude became most apparent at the dinner table, where Dominic and Ricardo made daily reports on their respective

areas of responsibility and presented various
courses of action for him to decide on—a continua-
tion of the tradition established by Ramon Valera.
Most of the time Fernando left the decisions up to
them. With Dominic this usually followed an attentive hearing and several shrewd, incisive questions,
whereas it was becoming Fernando's habit to dismiss Ricardo's problems almost before he'd heard
the man out. His behavior didn't seem to surprise
Eviana at all, but it puzzled Lee enormously. One
day she cornered her husband after dinner and
demanded to know why he habitually gave Ricardo
such short shrift.

Fernando shrugged. "Grain growing doesn't
excite me. Besides," he went on, "why should I
worry about it when Ricardo is ten times better
than I'll ever be at managing labor and increasing
the productivity of the land?"

His answer left Lee even more mystified than
before. She had steeled herself for the tension and
the flares of temper that might accompany Fernando's efforts to learn how to run the ranch. But she
wasn't sure how to cope with such stubborn
apathy. She started to fear that the Valera property
was destined to go the way of the many other
ranches Fernando had told her about—run by man-
agers and foremen while the owners took it easy.

The days slipped into a routine. Eviana, Fernando and Lee ate lunch together, then Lee and
Fernando would settle down with their coffee in
the salon or under one of the shade trees in the
garden to enjoy the fresh fragrance of springtime.
Eviana almost never joined them, preferring to
visit the cemetery or to read in her room. Her

attitude toward Lee hadn't changed; she was still polite, distant and unsmiling.

When Lee mentioned this to Fernando he immediately defended his sister. "She just doesn't know you very well yet. Give her a chance to open up to you. Eviana is like that. She either hates, loves or doesn't care—no halfway measures, no hypocrisy. I'm sure that if you made an effort to meet her halfway, everything would work out and you'd become good friends."

But Lee was unconvinced. Halfway meant Eviana had to try, too, and there seemed little evidence of effort on her part.

Toward the end of the afternoon, Fernando often headed out to the corrals. Sometimes Lee accompanied him, not wanting to remain alone in the house. But the only time she had her husband's undivided attention was in the evening, when they went back to their rooms. During the day, constantly surrounded by other people, he tended to be rather gruff and impersonal. And even when they were alone together, he wasn't the same attentive, gentle man anymore.

Lee had sensed it as soon as they left Madrid— Fernando had changed. The difference in him, moreover, grew more noticeable with each day that passed. She tried to persuade herself that it was caused by the heavy reponsibility he had so suddenly inherited. Sometimes, watching him without his knowledge, she thought he looked unhappy. Granted, there was the grief he was still suffering over his father's death, but there was also something else... the fleeting impression she had had that he was nervous and uneasy for some reason that she couldn't begin to fathom.

Eviana might know what was bothering him, Lee realized, if she could ever get through her sister-in-law's wall of politeness to ask. When Fernando abdicated his decision-making powers each evening at the dinner table, Eviana never intervened or commented, she never even looked worried. Lee knew that Eviana owned half the ranch. Did she really have that much confidence in Dominic's and Ricardo's ability?

Lee soon found that time was weighing heavily on her hands. The Valeras led a frankly idle existence, and since she didn't share their principal pastimes, it was up to her to fill the empty hours for herself. She sent Dominic to San Luis, therefore, to get her some wool and needlepoint canvas, as well as some books in both Spanish and English. She also did a little gardening when she felt up to it, but decided that her other hobbies—cooking and woodwork—would have to wait. She didn't want to risk affronting the staff at the *casa.* Lee was thankful when her trunks arrived, and she was able to decorate her room with some of the familiar and beloved treasures that had stood on her bedroom shelves back in Boston.

Fernando hadn't said anything more about renovations to their quarters, and she decided to wait a while longer before reminding him of his promise. Physical activity didn't particularly appeal to her just then, anyway. She often felt too tired to do even the things she enjoyed. And her appetite was so poor that not even Rosa's excellent cooking could tempt her. Strangely enough, or perhaps not strangely at all, Fernando and Eviana seemed oblivious to her run-down condition. But whenever she refused a dish at the dinner table, Lee would often turn to find Dominic's penetrating gaze on her face.

In the morning, when Fernando was customarily away, Lee would sometimes take brief strolls by herself. It was pleasant to ramble along a path that usually seemed to disappear just short of the next field. Gradually the vastness of the property was becoming familiar and comfortable to her, and she was becoming quite accustomed to the unified expanse of sun-drenched fields, which stretched all the way to the horizon, pushing their rows of wheat, corn and alfalfa sprouts toward the sky.

That was how she met the new *padre* one day, the only priest for more than thirty miles around. They encountered each other as he was returning from a walk with some young children from the village. When Lee introduced herself he smiled and offered her his hard, callused hand. The *padre* was evidently no stranger to manual labor.

"I'm Father Domingues. I'm delighted to meet you, *señora*," he said, "and I bless the luck that put me on your path. Otherwise, who knows when we might have met? When I first arrived, I visited all my parishioners to introduce myself, of course. But you and your husband were in Europe, I believe." She nodded. "Why the look of surprise?" he added, sensitive to the slight change in her expression.

Blushing, Lee admitted, "It's your hand. Here you are in your brown woolen robe with its rope sash, looking like a scholarly seminarian, and yet you have the hands of a...of a—"

"Of a carpenter?" he supplied with a grin. All at once the priest pulled up the skirt of his robe to reveal the frayed bottoms of a pair of blue work pants. "Some of my brethren believe in offering only spiritual assistance to their flocks," he explained, dropping his robe again as the chidren stared up at him in awe. "Following Jesus's example, however, I've always felt that a hammer is far superior to prayer when the roof needs fixing. That's why I'm also growing vegetables behind the presbytery. When the weather gets warmer I'll dispense with this robe and show myself in my true colors, so to speak."

Lee was certain that Fernando had neglected to pay even a courtesy visit to this energetic young priest, and the thought made her blush even more. If Father Domingues had been slighted by the omission she would have apologized on the spot, but he seemed to have dismissed it from his mind.

Just then the smallest of the children, a little boy with dark curly hair, tugged impatiently at the rope belt. Placing a calming hand on the boy's head and indicating the other youngsters in the restless group, the *padre* said, "Forgive me for cutting our conversation short, *señora,* but these children are hungry and I have to take them back to the village. I'm minding them today, since the schoolteacher is ill and these little ones have no one at home to look after them during the day."

On impulse Lee reached into her pocket and brought out a handful of pesetas, which she gave out to the delighted children. Then she stood thoughtfully for a moment, watching the shepherd lead his flock down the road.

FERNANDO AND HIS SISTER were riding back in comfortable silence toward the Casa Rosada. Between siblings as close as they were, there was no need to converse beyond a few short remarks.

"Let's cut through the village," Fernando suggested suddenly. "It's a more pleasant ride than the road."

Eviana glanced sharply at him. "This is getting to be a habit," she murmured, then let the matter drop.

In the village that day, as on all previous occasions when Eviana had ridden with him, Fernando's eyes sought out and held one particular cottage, its shutters half-closed, which was slightly recessed from the street. Geraniums were blossoming around the perimeter of the tiny garden, and a climbing rosebush cloaked the outhouse that marked the rearmost boundary of the property.

Suddenly one of the ranch jeeps screeched to a halt in front of the cottage. A young man leaped down with urgent grace and headed for the door.

"Well, well," Eviana remarked loudly. "It appears that Samantha had made a new conquest."

As Fernando watched the young man enter the cottage, he gripped Carioca's reins with whitened knuckles. In his eyes burned the flame of a murderous rage. Eviana frowned, waiting for an explosion, but she had underestimated his self-control. In a voice that sounded flat and contained, he asked, "Who is that?"

"I think his name is Hernandes. You don't know him. Ricardo hired him to assist in supervising the fields—with father's approval, of course—about two months ago. He tried to tell you about it at dinner the other day, but you wouldn't listen. I know how hard this Hernandes is willing to work, but I see he also likes to play...."

Fernando was staring unwaveringly at the Cartes residence, an unquenchable fire blazing in his eyes. "I wonder how he'll explain his presence here in the middle of the morning," he muttered between clenched teeth. Then, without warning, he spurred on his horse, leaving Eviana standing there as he galloped over to the cottage. Tying Carioca to the single tree in the front yard, he went and pounded on Samantha's door until she opened it.

She was clad in a light dress that clung to her curves like a second skin; her dark hair tumbled wildly over her shoulders. Hernandes stood directly behind her, was a handsome fellow with dark hair and complexion, perhaps twenty-five years old.

"What's your name?" Fernando demanded harshly.

"Orlando Hernandes," he replied, a little taken aback. Still, even though he probably knew the identity of the man confronting him, he retained his composure in front of Samantha. Tilting his chin defiantly, Hernandes met his employer's furious stare without flinching.

"You work under Ricardo Ruiz, isn't that right?"

"*Si, señor.*"

"What time is it, Hernandes?" Fernando asked, planting both hands on his hips.

Startled by the question, he glanced at his watch and replied, "It's a quarter past ten, *señor.*"

"What the hell are you doing in the village at this hour?" Fernando asked, his fury barely controlled.

"One of the *peons* put a pitchfork through his foot and Orlando had to drive him to Dr. Chandler's office for medical attention," Samantha broke in, her voice warm and musical in spite of the tension in the air. "While the doctor was looking after him, Orlando decided to come say hello—"

"You have no business being here, Hernandes," Fernando said, cutting her off. There was the ring of steel in his voice. "Go wait for the patient in Dr. Chandler's office. And if you value your job, don't come gallivanting into town again on my time."

The young man's hands formed fists at his sides but he didn't say anything in his defense. Instead he muttered goodbye to Samantha and left. Fernando heard the brief roar of the jeep's engine before Hernandes put it in gear and drove off. Meanwhile, he and Samantha stood glaring at each other.

"What gives you the right to burst in on me and chase my friends away?" she demanded angrily. There were two dots of flaming color on her cheeks and her eyes glittered like diamonds.

"When your friends are my employees, visiting you instead of working, then their conduct becomes my business," Fernando pointed out coldly. "You know you shouldn't be entertaining them at this hour of the day."

"I'll do whatever I please," she retorted. "And what goes on inside these four walls is none of your affair!"

"Except when you let yourself be courted by men who should be out in the fields, earning their pay," he growled.

Samantha's expression began to change slowly then, like ice melting. Her lovely mouth curved into a provocative smile. "If you hadn't come back from Europe with a wife I might believe that you were jealous of all the men who...court me. And by the way, congratulations. I hope you're as happy as any man deserves to be who builds his marriage on a lie!" Her smile faded as she spat the last word at him with a look of utter scorn.

Fernando grew pale. "You'd better watch what you say," he warned her coldly.

"What's the matter? Can't you take the truth?" she asked with a bitter laugh.

"There's no use making a scene, Samantha. What's done is done, and nothing can undo it."

She looked him carelessly up and down with her dark eyes still sparkling with anger. "You didn't have to come into my home and attack me, *señor*," she informed him in a brittle voice. "I would have stayed where you put me, in the place that I should never have dreamed of leaving and to which you should never have stooped in the first place. Now get out of my house! Get out and don't ever come back!"

Fernando opened his mouth to say something, but changed his mind. His face livid, he turned abruptly and left, followed out the door and onto the street by her enraged cry, "Don't ever come back! Never!"

Eviana hadn't moved from her spot. As her brother drew nearer and she saw his rigid expression, she asked curiously, "Was it a big fight?"

Fernando shrugged and consciously relaxed his features. "Of course not. I bawled out Hernandes and scolded Samantha, that's all. This evening I'm going to recommend to Ricardo that he keep an eye

on that fellow and not let him shirk his responsibilities."

"But you can't ask Ricardo to be a watchdog on
the actions of his second-in-command," Eviana protested. "He'll never get his own work done."

"Eviana, please. This is my affair."

"It's Samantha, isn't it?" she burst out hotly.
"You just can't bear the thought of anyone else—"

"Shut up! I don't have to take that kind of talk
from anyone!"

Eviana gave him a single, poisonous look, then
flicked her reins on the neck of her horse and trotted ahead of him.

THAT AFTERNOON, LEE TOLD FERNANDO about her
meeting with the *padre.* "The smallest boy was just
adorable," she added. "He had such huge dark eyes
and curly hair...."

But Fernando seemed unimpressed. "And I suppose he was covered with dirt as well," he sighed
disdainfully. "Those people have too many babies
and not enough time to care for them properly."

"Have the Valeras never thought of establishing
a nursery for the youngest ones?" Lee ventured.

"In this country we don't have welfare and family assistance, *querida.* However, father was always
an enlightened man. He shortened his employees'
work hours, paid them a decent wage and provided
comfortable lodging for their families. As for the
children, they have a school and a *padre.* What more
do they need?"

Obviously, it would take more than one conversation to make her husband see the light, Lee
thought. She abandoned the subject temporarily

and asked instead, "Darling, would you like to have a baby? Wouldn't you like to be a father?"

He shrugged indifferently. "Later, maybe. We have plenty of time.... For the moment there's something else I'd like to discuss with you. What would you say to making a grand tour of some of the typical regions of Argentina? We could leave right away."

"What?" she said faintly. It was such an enormous proposal, and he had thrown it at her so unexpectedly that she was at a loss for words.

Misunderstanding her silence he explained, "Right away is just a figure of speech, *querida*. You can have all the time you need to pack."

Lee's thoughts were churning dizzily. "You want to go on a vacation already? But you haven't even taken over the ranch yet...."

Fernando's features tensed with irritation. "I've already told you, Dominic and Ricardo can handle everything. Dominic is like one of the family, he can take my place."

"Then you intend to leave him and Eviana in charge of Casa Rosada?"

"No," he admitted. "I thought we could take Eviana with us. After all she's been through, she could use the change of scenery."

Lee frowned, not at all pleased with the prospect.

"Well?" he insisted. "What do you say?"

She opted for honesty. Putting her arms around his neck she gazed directly into his eyes and replied, "Two things are wrong with your plan. First of all, I love it here and don't particularly want to get away. And secondly, we're a newlywed couple and Eviana would feel like a fifth wheel if we dragged her all over the country with us."

Angrily, Fernando removed himself from her embrace and began to pace the room. "Then you refuse to make the trip if Eviana comes along, is that it?"

"Look, I've just told you what I think. Don't you agree? Or have you already lost interest in being alone with me?"

Reading the anxiety in Lee's eyes, he came back to her with open arms. "Of course I haven't," he assured her. "And you're probably right about Eviana. She would feel out of place." He was smiling, but Lee thought she caught an undercurrent of tension beneath his words, some pervasive shadow of discontent. "So we'll get away together, just you and I," he decided abruptly. "And I'll send Eviana to stay with our cousin Alexia. Does that suit you?"

Lee sighed. He hadn't heard her first objection to the trip and, in view of his obvious anxiety to escape from the ranch, she was reluctant to repeat it. Even though she hadn't the slightest desire to go searching for new horizons at that moment, she managed to give him a smile of approval. "It suits me fine," she said.

Immediately, Fernando seemed to come alive. He began chattering volubly about their trip. "We'll visit the northern provinces, in the district of Tucuman— the main crop up there is sugar cane—then we'll go on to Salta where they have the best preserved examples of colonial architecture. We'll cross to the Andes and see the descendants of the Incas in their colorful ponchos. Wait and see, *querida*, we'll recover the happiness we left behind in Europe."

On and on he talked, like someone who was trying to hide behind a wall of words.

"Why are you so anxious to leave?" Lee asked at last, her heart constricting with anguish. "Is it for the same reason you want Eviana to have different surroundings? Is it to learn to accept your father's death and to forget?"

Suddenly Fernando's face fell. After a pause he confessed in a harsh voice, "Yes, I want to try to forget."

Chapter 6

Whether because of worry or annoyance, Lee slept very poorly that night. Fernando was gone when she finally got up, feeling lightheaded and nauseous. Her stomach turned at the very sight of food, and after an unsuccessful attempt to have breakfast she was forced to tell Luisa apologetically, "I just can't eat this morning. Perhaps some tea...?"

"*Si, señora*. Rosa will make you a cup of *mate*."

Lee had heard about this tealike infusion, traditionally drunk by Argentinians through a straw. When it arrived at the table, strong and steaming in a gourd-shaped mug, it had already been liberally sugared. She set the silver straw aside and sipped in the conventional manner and, as she drained the last of the *mate*, she felt so much better that she decided to walk to the village, a mile and a quarter away. She had avoided making the trip until then, not because of the distance but because she dreaded the curiosity of the workers' families. Well, it was time she emerged from her cocoon.

Lee set off on foot right after breakfast. Half a

mile down the road she suddenly became aware of a
car coming up behind her, and moments later one
of the ranch jeeps rolled abreast of her and halted.
Dominic was at the wheel, scanning her with his
inscrutable hazel eyes.

"Are you going to the village?" he asked.

She nodded, not trusting herself to speak.

"That's where I'm going, too. Would you like a
lift?"

Lee hesitated. For a fleeting moment she wished
she had Fernando's effortless condescension
toward the ranch employees. Her husband would
view such an offer as the fulfillment of a natural
obligation, certainly not a favor that might have to
be repaid. But standing alone on that dusty road,
Lee felt like any hitchhiker. And Dominic, despite
the respect in his voice, wasn't looking at her as
though she were the *señora* of Casa Rosada.

The distance wasn't that far, she told herself, and
she was almost halfway there already.... Then a
wave of fatigue stole over her and she realized with
a pang of disappointment that she had little choice
but to accept the ride. Besides, there were storm
clouds on the horizon, and she would hate to get
caught in the rain this far from the *casa*.

When the jeep was rolling again, Lee asked, "Are
there any stores in the village?"

"I'm afraid they don't have real shops," he replied. "There's a sort of general store where the
villagers can get staple foodstuffs and dry goods—
nothing fancy, though. Apart from that, there's a
cafe where the men gather in the evening, a
Samiento school, the church and the few houses
that you can see over there."

"Then there isn't a drugstore?"

"No."

Lee suppressed a sigh of disappointment.

"To find a proper drugstore you'd have to go all the way into Santana," Dominic went on. "Fortunately, Dr. Chandler has a well-stocked dispensary. That's where I'm going today, in fact."

"I guess I'd better see him, too," she said quietly.

Dominic slowed the jeep and glanced at her in puzzled concern. "Are you ill?"

Lee forced herself to smile. "Oh, it's nothing serious.... But tell me about Dr. Chandler. That's not an Argentinian name. Who is he? Has he been here long?"

"Chandler is American, arrived about six years ago. He's a simple, straightforward man, sometimes brutally honest. But he's an excellent doctor, and he gives all his patients the same care, whether they can pay his fee or not. I like him, and I think he likes me. I'm driving over this morning to pay him for a medication he prepared for one of our colts."

Lee's eyes opened wide in surprise. "You mean he's a veterinarian?"

"No, but sometimes he helps me out because he's the only one around with any medical training."

"But surely he doesn't examine and prescribe for horses!"

Dominic threw back his head and laughed, and Lee was amazed at the transformation she saw in his features. Suddenly his face was youthful and open, even mischievous. "Not yet, he doesn't," he replied, and for a moment his eyes sparkled with amusement.

The jeep was rolling down the village's main

street, an unpaved road lined with cottages and ending at the church, which sat bathed in the morning light. At the third house before the church Dominic stopped the car, but he made no move to get out. Instead he turned and gazed into Lee's blue eyes.

"Before you decide whether to go in or not, I think you ought to know," he explained, "that for a long while now Dr. Chandler and the Valera family have not been on good terms. In fact, Eviana and your husband won't even talk to him."

"Can you tell me why?"

He shook his head. "Even if I was sure of the reason, it wouldn't be my place to discuss it."

Lee didn't press him. "Since it obviously happened before my time, I don't see how it involves me," she said with a dismissive gesture.

But the unreadable hazel eyes remained focused on her face. "I have to tell you one more thing. Chandler wouldn't mind my mentioning it because it's common knowledge, especially in a village as small as this one, where nothing is secret for long. When he first arrived, the doctor drank rather heavily, always behind closed doors. Nonetheless, word got out. Don't think because of that that he's a drunkard. Today he hardly touches a drop of alcohol."

Returning his stare, Lee frowned and said uncertainly, "It sounds as though you're trying to dissuade me, Dominic."

The foreman shrugged and shook his head. "I just think you should know the situation before you go in."

"And is there anything you've left out?" she asked, a smile beginning to tug at her lips.

"I don't think so."

"Fine. Then let's go see this notorious Dr. Chandler!"

In the school across the road, students were reciting the multiplication tables in a loud chorus of childish voices. Except for that, Lee might have thought the village was deserted, for the streets were strangely empty.

Dominic knocked at the doctor's door. A moment later a voice shouted from within, and Dominic turned the knob and ushered Lee into a large vestibule lined with rough wooden benches.

She heard the scraping of a chair in the next room and a man suddenly appeared in the doorway: He ws tall and quite thin and looked about fifty years old. His face wasn't lined, but rather stamped with a disillusioned expression. When he saw Lee his jaw dropped in astonishment.

"If I'm not mistaken, You are the new *señora* of Casa Rosada!" he exclaimed in heavily-accented Spanish.

To Lee's immeasurable relief, Dominic interceded at that moment. "The *señora* wanted to see you and, since I was coming this way anyway, I brought her along. Here's your fee, doctor," he said, holding out an envelope. Then, turning to Lee, he added, "I'll wait outside in the jeep for you."

"You don't have to, Dominic," Lee replied hastily. "But thanks anyway."

With a wave the foreman was gone, closing the front door behind him. Dr. Chandler showed Lee into the austere room that served as his office. Then, indicating a seat, he said, "Forgive my surprise at your unexpected visit, *señora*, but I haven't seen a member of the Valera family in quite a while—except for Dominic, of course. When the Valeras are ill, they usually send for a specialist from Santana or San Luis. The one time they called on me for anything serious, the patient was beyond my help."

"I know about that," Lee told him in English.

"Let's speak Spanish, *señora*, if you don't mind. I don't want to start any more rumors," Chandler remarked curtly, thrusting his hands deep into his pockets. "Does your husband know you're here?"

"No."

He made a wry face. "I thought as much. Very well, let's not prolong your stay. Tell me to what I owe the pleasure of this visit, *señora* Valera."

So far the doctor's remarks had been abrasive to the point of rudeness, but Lee refused to be irritated. "I want you to examine me," she said simply.

Chandler stared at her incredulously. "Did I hear you correctly? You want an examination?"

She nodded. "For some time now I've been having spells of nausea and dizziness. I thought I ought to see a doctor."

With a deepening frown, he gazed into her face. "Dominic has probably told you that I've been here for six years, treating the villagers. But are you aware of the hostility that exists between the Valeras and me?"

"Yes."

As he shook his head slowly his bitter expression relaxed. Chandler walked thoughtfully around the room, drawing Lee's eyes from the desk to the examining table to the glass-doored cabinet filled with apothecary bottles. Then he sat down across the desk from her and said contritely, "I must ask you to forgive the way I behaved just now."

Lee smiled. "Consider yourself forgiven. I think I can understand how a person could become disenchanted living out here."

Her frankness may have surprised Chandler but it didn't displease him. "It sounds as if the doctor needs a doctor," he remarked wryly.

"But please remember that I'm the patient this morning," she rejoined, still smiling.

"Fair enough, and I want you to know that I appreciate your bringing your medical problem to me, in spite of the low opinion your people have of my professional abilities."

Lee was shocked. "Why? Because you care for the *peons* and their families?"

He smiled faintly. "That's part of it. When I first arrived, I tried to conceal my past, thinking that it was nobody's business but mine. That was a mistake. The half-truths that circulated about me were far more damaging than the truth might have been. Soon the village housewives were gossiping about how I'd been dismissed from my post as chief of medicine of a large hospital in Chicago because of some flagrant dereliction of my professional duty. So the Valeras refused to call on me. I was good enough for their *peons*, but not for them."

"But surely once you'd set the record straight . . . ."

"It made no difference," Chandler shrugged fatalistically. "Ramon Valera was a hardheaded old man who refused to back down once he'd made up his mind about anything, and he'd already decided that I was a second-rate doctor."

He'd left the truth behind the rumors tantalizingly unspoken, but discretion kept Lee from asking questions.

"I gather you don't share his judgment," Chandler added with a crooked smile.

"I never met my late father-in-law, so I had no opportunity to be influenced by him."

"Tell me about this nausea, *señora*," he asked suddenly, pulling a manila folder out of a desk drawer and printing the name Valera across it in block letters.

"It comes and goes, but it's worst in the morning. The sight of food turns my stomach lately."

"And you mentioned dizziness. Does this accompany the nausea?"

"Most of the time, although sometimes I feel just plain dizzy and tired."

A smile was creeping across Chandler's face. Turning to a steel cabinet Lee hadn't noticed before, he pulled a cylindrical plastic container out of a drawer. "If you could put a urine specimen in there for me, *señora*.... It's not as definitive a test as the one done with frogs or rabbits, but if it comes out positive, I'll probably have some good news for you."

Thirty minutes later Lee was standing outside on the street, not noticing or caring that the entire sky had become dark and threatening. The test had proved positive, and all her suspicions were now a certainty. Her malaise and weariness had a specific cause—she was two months preganant.

Chandler's words were still ringing in her ears: "You have to take care of youself and not do anything stupid. If this were Chicago I wouldn't have to make this recommendation, but we're out in the wilderness here, far from paved roads, so I want you to avoid long automobile rides. You're a little anemic and run-down, but you ought to carry to term and deliver without difficulty if you just use common sense...."

Slowly Lee felt a glow of joy swelling inside her. Never had she felt so alive. Her awareness of her body had increased tenfold in the last half hour, until every inch of her skin seemed to tingle as she walked, caressed by the clothing she was wearing.

Just then she noticed the jeep parked at the corner of the street. Dominic was leaning against the hood of the car, watching her approach. She knew she was probably grinning like an idiot, but she didn't care.

"You didn't have to wait for me," she told him. "I could have walked back."

"I had nothing urgent to do this morning," he assured her.

On the way back to Casa Rosada, Dominic suddenly asked, "What do you think of Dr. Chandler?"

"I like him." Then it dawned on Lee that here was an opportunity to satisfy her curiosity, and she added, "Was it because he drank that he lost his post as chief of medicine?"

Dominic glanced at her before replying, "He told you about that, eh? Yes. He couldn't keep his professional and his personal lives separate. He had problems...so he began to drink. The board of the hospital was about to demand his resignation when he got an invitation to visit his brother, a priest in San Luis. Here in Argentina, Dr. Chandler was able to put himself back together, and when his brother was summoned about a year ago to a high ecclesiastical post in Cordoba, he decided to stay here, where his 'practice' was."

It wasn't until he was negotiating the turn into the driveway of the Casa Rosada that Dominic asked the question that must have been on his mind. "Was Dr. Chandler able to help you?"

Lee blushed. "Yes. I have to go back and see him again...."

"Nothing serious, I hope?"

"Nothing serious."

After a thoughtful pause, Dominic wondered aloud, "How do you suppose Fernando will react when he learns that you were examined by Dr. Chandler?"

"Once I've spoken to him about it, he'll take it very well," Lee stated, smiling with confidence.

Chapter 7

That morning being a Saturday, the outbuildings were almost deserted, and Samantha had been able to watch from her hiding place as Fernando, then Lee and finally Dominic left the ranch. She sighed as Dominic rode past her in the jeep—if only he had paid her a bit of attention, she thought, things might have turned out differently. But Dominic was serious-minded and reserved, and apparently not romantically entangled anywhere in the district. Was there perhaps a woman waiting for him in San Luis or Buenos Aires, where he often had to go on ranch business?

Samantha wandered over to the stables, where her father and two other men were preparing to foal a mare. Uttering a surprised exclamation, Julian Cartes took his daughter aside, with worried glances over his shoulder at the stable hands.

"I'd like to go for a ride, father," she said.

"You haven't ridden in weeks," he pointed out uneasily.

"I haven't had time."

A distant rumble of thunder caused them both to look up at the sky. "You've chosen a bad day, Samantha. It's going to rain."

"I don't care. A little bit of water doesn't frighten me."

Since she was obviously determined to go riding, Julian decided to level with her. "Samantha, the Señor Valera who permitted us to ride his horses whenever we pleased is dead. Before we assume that the privilege is still extended to us, I'd better talk to Señor Fernando or Señor Dominic. Otherwise I might be called up on the carpet for taking liberties...."

"Oh, please, father!" she begged. "Let me ride this morning. If anyone objects, I'll take all the responsibility."

Julian Cartes was reluctant to yield to his daughter's whim, especially in view of the threatening storm, but one of the stable hands summoned him just then, disrupting his train of thought. The foal was being born.

"All right," he muttered hastily to Samantha. "Take Tampico. And be careful."

A few minutes later, Samantha was galloping away from the Casa Rosada, bent over the golden mane of the proud white horse on which she'd learned to ride years ago. Her father sighed as he heard her pass. Under his tutelage she'd become a fine horsewoman, but that had been all he'd ever been able to teach her. For the most part, his daughter had followed her own fiercely independent heart.

LOST IN THOUGHT, Fernando let his horse wander

through the fields. All around him land was being broken to expand the Valeras' cultivated acreage, but the next year's alfalfa crop was the last thing on his mind just then.

Suddenly a drop of rain splashed onto his wrist. Fernando glanced up at the roiling, slate-colored sky and pulled at Carioca's reins, turning the horse onto the usual route home—cross-country and through the village. Carioca knew the way by himself. His master's gaze was free to roam over the passing countryside. Suddenly, out of the corner of his eye, Fernando saw something move and, turning slightly, he saw a saddled but riderless horse standing alone near a clump of shrubbery.

Intrigued, he decided to investigate, for he'd recognized the animal's unmarked white coat and golden mane and tail immediately. It was Tampico, a spirited stallion that his father had placed at the disposal of the Cartes family for whenever they wanted to ride. Not until Carioca had rounded the bushes did Fernando notice the body stretched out on the ground. "Samantha!" he shouted.

In a flash Fernando had dismounted and was racing toward her inert form. She appeared to be unconscious, but bore no apparent sign of injury.

"Samantha!" he cried again, carefully lifting her head. "Samantha! Answer me! Say something!"

Slowly her eyes opened.

"Are you hurt?" he demanded.

"My arm and my right leg...." she stammered.

"What happened?"

"I fell. I don't know how...."

"Give me your hand. See if you can sit up."

Suddenly she was leaning on one elbow, glaring

coldly at him. "Leave me alone. I don't need anybody," she snapped.

"Don't be stupid," he commanded her. And without giving her a chance to raise any further objections he began to pull her to her feet.

Her face twisted in pain and she gasped, "My ankle...and my wrist feels broken."

"Well, there's no swelling yet," he told her, after a cursory look at her ankle and wrist. "Do you think you could ride to the village?"

Samantha shook her dark head. "I don't think so. I'd be grateful if you'd go tell my father what's happened," she said, her voice stiff and proud. "He'll come and take me home."

It was beginning to rain.

"I'll take you home," Fernando said decisively.

"What, you'd let me double up on your horse?" she retorted sarcastically.

"Why not?" he retorted. "It's no crime to help out when someone is hurt." With that he lifted her easily in his arms, deposited her gently on Carioca's back and swung himself up in the saddle behind her.

The rain was splashing down in large drops. It was a shower that should have cooled his ardor, but Fernando still felt a surge of desire as her supple body pressed warmly against his chest and the perfume of her hair filled his nostrils. Tampico had drawn near and Fernando bent down to capture his reins. Leading the horse behind him, he headed toward the village, glancing anxiously at the black sky as he rode.

By the time they came to a halt in front of Samantha's cottage, the storm had broken, hurling opaque, gray sheets of water down on the riders. The main street of the village was gloomy and deserted as Fernando jumped down from his horse, soaked to the skin, his dark hair releasing rivulets of water down both sides of his face. His eyes were riveted in fascination on Samantha, who had never looked so lovely. Her blouse clung semitransparently to her ripe curves, bringing a sudden hoarseness to his voice as he invited her to dismount.

"My ankle is hurting me," she said plaintively. "It will never support my weight."

Gripping her by the waist, Fernando lowered her gently to the ground. Samantha groaned as her right foot contacted the packed earth, and he immediately swung her into his arms and carried her to the door. But before he could turn the knob she reminded him coldly, "I told you I never wanted you inside my house again."

With a dark look at his beautiful burden, he kicked the door open, carried her directly into her bedroom and set her down on the bed.

"I'll go get Dr. Chandler," he said.

Then, to his amazement, Samantha sprang lithely to her feet and tossed her damp hair back over her shoulders. "That won't be necessary." Suddenly her eyes were electrically charged velvet. "You see," she confessed, both her voice and manner provocative, "I didn't really fall off my horse. I just wanted to see whether you still had any feeling for me.... Now I know. You can leave, if that's what you really want to do."

For a long moment the rain continued to beat against the windowpane, its unvarying rhythm adding to the tension in the little room. Then, without a word, Fernando turned the key in the lock of Samantha's front door.

IN SPITE OF HER IMPATIENCE, Lee waited until after lunch, when they were alone together in their rooms, to break the happy news to Fernando. In a voice resonant with emotion she announced, "Darling, I'm going to have a baby."

He started violently, as though stung.

"It *is* a surprise, isn't it?" Lee laughed softly.

But not a pleasant one, obviously, she thought, dismayed by her husband's reaction. Instead of rushing over to gather her in a joyous embrace, he stood stock-still, his expression one of confused numbness until his brow furrowed in a dark scowl.

Lee stopped smiling. "Fernando? Aren't you going to say anything?"

"You knew, didn't you?" he said, his voice ragged with contained anger. "That's why you were talking about babies yesterday. Why didn't you say something then?"

"I—I wasn't sure. I only suspected ..." she faltered.

"And how can you be sure today?"

"Because I went to see Dr. Chandler this morning."

"Chandler! That's crazy!" Fernando's entire face had twisted in rage, and Lee felt her heart sink.

"Why? Isn't he as good a doctor as any other?"

"Not when he refuses to come see certain patients," Fernando declared.

"But he came when Eviana sent for him. She said herself that it was too late—"

"I'm not talking about that," he cut her off with a

scythlike gesture. "The man's a quack, Lee. And why didn't you talk to me before running off to see him? Didn't you think the father of your child should have some say in the matter?"

Tears were welling hotly in Lee's eyes. "Fernando, please, don't be angry. Not today. I wanted to surprise you with the news. I thought you'd be happy...."

"It was a stupid thing to do!" he fumed. "The news would have been just the same if we'd called in a specialist from San Luis. In any case, you're not going back to Chandler."

Forgetting her disappointment, she bridled at this display of authoritarianism. "Why not? Why should I adopt the quarrels of the Valera family and snub a man who's done me no harm?"

"Because you're my wife, Lee."

"Even if I disagree with an attitude that stems solely from your father's stubborn pride?"

"I see Chandler told you his side of the story, whitewashing himself, no doubt."

"He was very objective," she replied defiantly. "I'm afraid I can't say the same for you and Eviana."

"The matter was settled long ago, and I forbid you to return to his office," Fernando decreed once more, but Lee wasn't about to give in.

"What specifically did he do to turn the whole family against him?" she demanded.

"Soon after he arrived in the village, Eviana had a stomachache. We sent for him, but he refused to come. He was looking after the daughter of some *peon* and he refused to come!" Fernando roared.

"What if the child was terribly ill?" Lee countered. "If you were a doctor, wouldn't you stay by the bedside of the patient who needed you most?"

"How could he know which one that was, since he refused to come to examine Eviana?"

"I'm sure that if he had had any doubt about the seriousness of your sister's case, he would have rushed right over," Lee maintained stubbornly.

"*Querida*, I'll tell you once more that the question has been settled once and for all. Besides, Chandler's checkered past—"

"He's been the victim of rumors!" she cried.

"I wonder who put that idea into your head," Fernando remarked dryly. "It wouldn't surprise me if Dominic had been touting him, since I already know that they're fast friends."

Instinctively wanting to keep Dominic uninvolved, Lee said defiantly, "I don't need anyone else to make up my mind for me."

"I think it's scandalous that you visited that charlatan—it's humiliating for the entire family. From now on we'll send for a doctor from Santana or San Luis whenever you need one. And if you don't want to have the baby in a hospital, a specialist can come deliver it here."

It was pointless to argue with Fernando. He was as proud and stubborn as his father. Wearily, Lee sank into a chair, aching with disappointment. This should have been a moment of shared tenderness, but instead he had perverted it into a quarrel. And her husband's obvious indifference to the baby had been a cruel shock.

As he paced the room, Fernando tossed an angry question at her. "I suppose this means our trip is cancelled?"

"I'm afraid so," she replied tentatively. "In my

condition, on these roads...." She concluded with a shrug. His eyes hardened but he didn't say anything. "You never wanted this baby, did you?" Lee asked, her heart leaden.

"I just wasn't expecting it, that's all."

Suddenly the tears that had been building in her eyes could be contained no longer. As they spilled down her cheeks he snapped impatiently at her, "Lee, for the love of God, stop looking so tragic."

Just then there was a knock at the door. It was Luisa, delivering a message from Dominic: a buyer had arrived to look over the two colts that were for sale.

"Dominic should be able to handle something like that without me," he muttered, but Lee saw relief on his face as he turned to follow the servant down the stairs.

WHEN HE HAD RETURNED from the corral, Fernando closeted himself in his father's office. Lee didn't know what he was doing there and hardly cared anymore. Fernando, she realized, was stubborn, immovable and more concerned with his pride than with anyone else's feelings.

So it was a double shock that evening at dinner when Fernando ordered Rosa to fetch a bottle of fine vintage wine from the cellar. After opening it himself and filling all the wineglasses at the table, he announced, "We're drinking to the coming birth of a new Valera heir!"

There was an exchange of stunned looks, and then all eyes turned to Lee, who fidgeted uncomfortably in her seat, her cheeks flaming. Ricardo was the first to offer congratulations. Then Eviana followed suit, as did Dominic, who had suddenly understood the meaning of Lee's visit to Dr. Chandler and was frowning thoughtfully at her.

"Let's drink to the son who will grace the Casa Rosada before winter sets in," Fernando said, lifting his glass. "For I hope it is a son, to carry on the Valera name and the Valera tradition." He gave a significant glance at Lee. Downing his wine in large gulps, he refilled his goblet and proposed another toast, seeming to Lee to be determined to get drunk that evening. "Go on, have a little wine," he ordered his wife, gesturing toward her untouched glass. "It'll put color back into your cheeks."

Not wanting to anger him she wet her lips with the sweet wine, but it left the taste of ashes in her mouth.

Chapter 8

Three weeks went by. Lee had written to her
mother telling her that she was pregnant, but had
received no reply. Her parents' silence didn't weigh
as heavily on her mind, however, as did the drastic
change in her husband's temperament. Fernando's
moods had been swinging wildly lately, from a sort
of withdrawn moroseness to forced joviality, and
he occasionally exploded with a senseless anger
that disturbed and puzzled everyone around him.
Unable to understand such extreme behaviour, Lee
could only bear with it and hope that the storm
would soon subside. Bolstered by the thought of
the baby growing inside her, she waited patiently
for her husband to adjust to his new role as head of
the Valera household. For what else could possibly
be causing his moodiness, she wondered.

Inevitably, Lee's attempts to cope with Fernando's irrational outbursts began taking their toll.
Her physical condition had greatly improved,
thanks to Dr. Chandler's advice, but there were
days when she verged on depression. She hadn't

raised the issue with her husband again, but she intended to return to Chandler for her next monthly checkup. When she didn't follow his instructions to the letter she tired very easily. And she felt that in case of an emergency he would be the one they'd call anyway.

Meanwhile, the announcement of Lee's pregnancy seemed to have overcome Eviana's indifference to her new sister-in-law, although most of her attentions took the form of warnings not to exert herself. "You mustn't go running up and down the stairs, Lee! Rosa and Luisa are here, and they can fetch whatever it is you need."

A little surprised by this show of concern, Lee made a special effort to be amiable toward Eviana. But the girl still lacked the spontaneity of genuine feelings. Not sensing any true affection in Eviana, therefore, Lee found it difficult to respond. Rosa had shown her more warmth, Dr. Chandler more genuine concern. Even the enigmatic Dominic had demonstrated, at times, a sincere interest that Lee waited for in vain from Evaina.

Resigned to letting Fernando gallop through the countryside, alone or with his sister, and wanting to stay reasonably close to the house, Lee had found herself drawn more and more frequently to the corrals. She found it was an education just to stand and watch the wranglers handling the powerful animals. Dominic welcomed her interest, and was quite willing to talk at length about the various stages of a horse's life, as well as the work involved in maintaining a healthy herd. Over the weeks he taught her to know and love horses, even though she couldn't ride them.

But Dominic himself was still a puzzle. Granted, the more time they spent together, the less dramatic became the effect of his intense hazel eyes. Eventually she no longer felt her knees weaken or her throat become dry when she was with him. But that didn't make his gaze any less piercing, or his features any more revealing than before. Lee had stopped believing that his passiveness was a mask—evidently it was a natural attribute. But every time she was ready to concede that the foreman's soul concealed no poetry or passion, she would surprise a glimmer of something, a fleeting emotion in the depths of his eyes or at the corners of his mouth that would, once again, set her wondering about the man.

And when she wasn't puzzling over Dominic Fontanera, there was Julian Cartes. The grooms and stable boys were a friendly lot, always calling out and waving to her when she came over to the stables. But Julian Cartes made such a point of avoiding her that she felt compelled to remark on his strange behavior to Dominic one day. "I don't think Julian wants me around the stable. He avoids me studiously, refusing even to say hello unless he's cornered."

"Julian is a diamond in the rough," Dominic replied. "Sometimes his manners leave something to be desired, but I'm sure he doesn't mean anything by it."

Thoughtfully Lee watched the old man disappear behind the tack shed. "It's very strange, but I get the impression that he's hiding something."

"I really think you're imagining things," Dominic told her. Then he changed the subject. But a moment later she turned and found his grave hazel eyes on her, filled with compassion. She had a tremendous urge to demand an explanation, but then she told herself resolutely that she didn't dare.

That evening at dinner, the question of Julian Cartes came up again. Since Ramon Valera's death, Casa Rosada had gradually been dropping old practices. Whether from lack of interest or lack of competence, Fernando had stopped asking his foremen questions, and Ricardo's and Dominic's reports had been becoming increasingly brief. After both men had reported that night, Dominic said to Fernando, "Julian Cartes would like to know whether he and his daughter can continue to ride Tampico when they wish, as in the past."

Lee couldn't help noticing how attentively the others waited for Fernando's reply. Eviana, in particular, seemed to be straining to catch his every word.

"Why not?" Fernando said, staring down at his plate. "Nothing has changed around here."

Ordinarily Eviana didn't interfere in business discussions between her brother and the two foremen, but this time she broke in angrily. "How can you say that? Father was the one who accorded that privilege to the Cartes's, and we're under no obligation to maintain it."

"I see no reason to cut them off," her brother retorted.

Eviana sank back in her seat with a disgruntled expression. And from then on, the sight of Samantha galloping across the fields on her white charger with the golden mane and tail became almost a daily occurrence.

CARMELA MENDOZA'S WEDDING DAY was blessed with a cloudless sky. Eviana's eyes sparkled with satisfaction as she stood on the front step waiting for Ricardo to pick her up. Because she was in mourning, she wouldn't be able to attend anything but the religious ceremony, but even that event would give her several hours alone in Ricardo's company, driving to and from San Luis.

"You really do look very elegant," she greeted Ricardo with a smile, as he got out of the sports car Fernando had placed at their disposal. The foreman was wearing a well-tailored suit that made him look like a prosperous young executive instead of a hardworking rancher.

He, in turn, nodded appreciatively at the simple black dress and the single strand of pearls that she wore. "And you are exquisite, Eviana. You have real class." It was true that without being exceptionally tall or beautiful, Eviana had an innate grace and a proud carriage that belied her years, giving her a natural distinction. But Ricardo's compliment seemed to displease her.

"Never mind about 'class'!" she said with an impatient shrug.

"A foreman is a foreman and a princess is a princess," he pointed out evenly.

"I don't understand what pleasure it gives you to keep running yourself down," she said, as they headed for the car. "Men have risen to greatness from lowlier positions than yours. Using their intelligence, their strong will and self-confidence, some have become world leaders."

"You're talking about geniuses or opportunists who have taken advantage of extraordinary circumstances and have had a great deal of luck. I haven't got their ambition."

Before getting into the car Eviana smiled winningly at him. "I'm not asking you to be a statesman."

Ricardo decided to laugh. "That's good, because I'd certainly let you down." He got behind the wheel and they were off.

At the main gate of the ranch, he had to slow down to let Lee, who was out for a walk, cross the road. They responded to her wave, then Ricardo stepped hard on the accelerator. "Does she know?" he asked abruptly.

Even though she understood immediately what he was getting at, Eviana asked, "What do you mean?"

"I'm just wondering whether your sister-in-law knows where her husband has been spending his mornings," Ricardo said bluntly.

A remark like that coming from anyone else would have shocked Eviana and made her feel ashamed. But with Ricardo she didn't try to deny her brother's clandestine activity. "She doesn't know, and I hope she never finds out."

"Oh? Have you decided you like her after all?"

"Why should I feel anything for a stranger I hardly know? It takes time to judge and appreciate a person. After all, Lee could be a cunning opportunist, joining the family purely for financial reasons. I know that Fernando told father in one of his letters that she came from a rather poor family."

"If, as you claim, you need time to form an opinion of her, why suspect her immediately of having ulterior motives?"

"It isn't a suspicion, just a supposition," she corrected him. "And what do *you* think of her?"

"If she truly loves her husband, it's a pity he's giving her such a runaround. There must be plenty of men in the world who would devote their lives to guaranteeing the happiness of such a charming woman."

Eviana glanced sharply at him, then asked in a bantering tone, "And would you be among them, if she were free?"

Ricardo laughed lightly. "Who knows? If she comes from a poor family, she might be more accessible to someone like me."

Eviana's eyes narrowed. "Listen," she said suddenly, "Fernando might be being unfaithful to Lee, but she's still his legal wife, and any other man who dared to cast loving eyes at her wouldn't have a hope. She's expecting a Valera baby. That's what concerns me, and that's why I want her pregnancy to run smoothly until the day she delivers. Afterward...." She shrugged, then changed the subject.

The trip to San Luis seemed very short. As they were approaching the outskirts of the city, Eviana suddenly turned to Ricardo and said, "I want you to come into the church with me and attend the mass."

Keeping his eyes on the road, he answered calmly, "No, that wouldn't be wise. What would your friends think if they ever found out who I was?"

"I have no intention of hiding the truth from them."

"That would be insane. If your brother ever heard of it—"

"My brother has no right to sit in judgment on me," she declared sharply. "It would be a case of the pot calling the kettle black."

Suddenly Ricardo's expression darkened. He stepped on the brakes and pulled over onto the shoulder of the road. Shutting off the ignition, he turned toward her angrily. "Listen, Eviana, you'd better find some other way to challenge your brother's authority. I want to keep my job."

"Fernando wouldn't dare fire you," Eviana insisted. Then she seemed to melt against the seat, and in a silken voice she went on, "Look at me, Ricardo! You're the one I want to spend the rest of my life with, and I refuse to pay lip service to any antiquated notions of so-called propriety. If you feel the same way, if you want more than anything else to have me as your wife, nothing will stand in your way, I promise!"

Ricardo laughed and started the car again. "You'd tempt the devil himself. We'd better get going, otherwise you might turn my head."

As the sports car skimmed along the road toward the center of San Luis, Ricardo kept the rest of his thoughts to himself, infuriating his passenger no end. Not another word was exchanged until the majestic tower of San Francisco Church was in sight. "I'll drop you at the church and come back for you after the ceremony," Ricardo told her. "I have something to do in town."

"Going to visit a girl friend?" she inquired dryly.

"I want to pick up some brochures on a new agricultural machine to show your brother," he assured her with a condescending smile.

EARLY THAT SAME AFTERNOON, in a travesty of their former intimacy, Lee and Fernando had settled into the salon to have a cup of *mate*. Fernando was showing a more pleasant side of himself, although Lee was sensitive to the effort it took him to maintain that appearance. His moods were becoming volatile in the extreme and, paradoxically, there was for Lee a certain constancy to that volatileness. She knew to expect the unexpected: he could switch in the blink of an eye from pleasant to surly, from charming to indifferent.

Even though Fernando often inquired after his wife's health, he studiously avoided talking about the impending birth of their child. For this reason, Lee had decided not to mention her next visit to Dr. Chandler.

Fernando was taking longer and longer to come in from his morning rides, and she supposed that he was finally taking an interest in the management of the ranch. As the days passed, however, Lee's thoughts dwelled more and more on the baby, until the future became all-important. Caught up in her incipient motherhood, she noticed in passing that Samantha was avoiding her as scrupulously as Julian was, but she wasted no time wondering where the linen maid was going each time she galloped past the house on Tampico. The present had simply lost significance for Lee.

That afternoon, Fernando took a letter out of his pocket and handed it to his wife. Lee scanned the message, which was written in a strong, elegant hand. It had come from Fernando's cousin, Alexia. She and her husband were anxious to meet their new relative, and were inviting all three Valeras to visit on a day that was convenient for them.

"Forgive the delay in sending this invitation," Alexia had written, "but the children, especially the baby, have been taking up all of my time. Eviana can tell you that I refuse to delegate the raising of my children to anyone, with the occasional exception of my mother-in-law. I also thought it would be better to let some time pass after the grievous loss we've all just suffered." She concluded by asking for a rapid reply and assuring the Valeras of her affection.

Lee wanted to meet Alexia and her family very much, but they lived almost sixty miles from Casa Rosada. "And the road is in bad shape," Fernando pointed out. "So you probably won't want to make the trip in a car."

In fact, Lee wanted to avoid all risks. "Why don't we just reverse the invitation?" she suggested. "I'm sure that when she knows I'm pregnant she'll understand why I can't travel that distance, and will be glad to come here instead."

Fernando agreed at once. "Will you reply to her note then?"

"I'll do it this afternoon. Tell me a little about Alexia...."

"She's our only first cousin, the daughter of my father's brother Felipe. Jorge, her husband, runs the corn cannery she inherited when Uncle Felipe died a few years ago. He comes from an excellent family, works as if he had to do it for a living, and thinks of nothing but making a profit," Fernando concluded with a note of scorn in his voice.

Just then Luisa appeared at the door to tell Fernando that Dominic wanted to talk to him.

It was unusual for Dominic to speak to Fernando about the farm at any other time except dinner. When he entered the room, he greeted Lee briefly, and then said to Fernando, "Forgive this interruption, but it was urgent that I talk to you." He glanced anxiously at Lee, as though reluctant to speak in front of her.

Ignoring the signal, Fernando snapped impatiently, "Talk! I'm listening!"

With a sigh the foreman went on, "Yesterday you signed a bill of sale for three horses. This morning while you were gone, one of the horses hurt his leg badly enough that he can't be sold. The buyer came thirty minutes ago for his horses. I explained the situation to him, and he agreed to accept another horse in place of the wounded one. He picked Tampico. Julian agreed, and so I took it upon myself to give him Tampico instead."

"Why Tampico?" Fernando snapped.

"Why not Tampico?" the foreman rejoined. "The problem is that Samantha arrived just in time to see him being loaded into the buyer's trailer. She raised a fuss, claiming that you've given her unlimited riding privileges on Tampico. Will you please come and settle this business?"

Suddenly Fernando's voice was crisp and metallic. "What the hell did Julian think he was doing, getting mixed up in this? And as for you, who gave you permission to do business without consulting me first?"

Dominic's face grew pale, and Lee guessed that he was exercising considerable self-control. "Some time ago you gave me full authority to sell off our horses before they grew old and lost their value," he reminded his employer in a frosty voice.

"You've given me hardly any information about these transactions."

"You've never asked for any. I thought there was nothing wrong with letting the buyer choose his own replacement."

"It's not your place to think for me!" Fernando roared.

"Please, Fernando, calm down," Lee begged her husband, afraid of what might happen if Dominic lost his temper. He'd have every right to do so, for Fernando was being cruelly unfair. "What does it matter if Tampico is sold? There are plenty of riding horses in the corrals—"

"I didn't want to sell that horse!"

"But why? You've never shown any particular attachment toward him, and I can't imagine that you'd let Samantha's objections influence you in a business matter."

Fernando's jaw muscles were tense. Finally he pushed away his cup of *mate* and poured himself a shot glass of whiskey, which he drained in a single gulp. "I have my reasons and they're nobody's business," he declared with suppressed violence. "Tampico stays here!"

"In that case, you'd better come and explain that to the buyer yourself. He's waiting by the stables," Dominic rejoined.

"If I have to smooth things over after your mistake, when you never had the authority to make the decision in the first place, then you're a bloody incompetent!"

"Fernando!" Lee was on her feet in indignation at her husband's unfairness. She'd heard him complain many times—groundlessly—that Dominic and Ricardo lacked initiative and decisiveness. But never had she seen him accuse either of them—to their faces—with such blatant unjustness.

"This is business, Lee, and doesn't concern you at all," he said, glaring at her.

"I disagree. You're behaving like a petty tyrant. How dare you berate Dominic that way! He isn't some *peon* that you can humiliate whenever you please!"

"Lee, please—"

"I'll have my say!" she declared hotly. "It's irrational and totally unfair of you to reproach this man, when you've asked him twenty times at least to stop bothering you with minor details and learn to handle his responsibilities!"

Being dressed down in Dominic's presence only increased Fernando's rage, and he told Dominic in a menacing undertone, "My father made the mistake of treating you like a son. Well, I intend to change all that. You'll have to deal with me from now on!" He got up, pushing his chair back so forcefully that it clattered to the floor. Then he stormed out, slamming the door behind him.

Sighing helplessly, Lee turned toward Dominic and said in embarrassment, "You'll have to forgive him. I don't understand this sudden fury over a horse."

Dominic looked uncomfortable. "I'm just sorry you got involved," he told her.

"Are you angry with me for defending you?"

"Not at all. But I wouldn't want to cause arguments between you and your husband."

"It's not you, Dominic," she replied sadly. "You

mustn't hate him. The sudden death of his father
has changed his character."

"That's what it must be," Dominic murmured,
and left the room.

Chapter 9

Nobody knew whether Fernando won or lost by it, but he reached an agreement with the buyer and Tampico stayed. As Samantha stood gloating over her victory, he commanded her in a low voice to go home and not show her face at Casa Rosada for several days. "I'll come and see you," he promised.

That evening, silence reigned around the dinner table. Dominic stared at his plate. Lee picked at her food absently, lost in her private thoughts, while Ricardo looked thoughtfully at the pair of them, noting their strained expressions.

Unaware of the storm that had raged during her absence, and oblivious to the tensions at the table, Eviana sat daydreaming about her friend Carmela's happiness, and about the time she'd spent in Ricardo's company. On the way home he had been friendly enough, but at no time had he dropped his guard and spoken to her with any kind of intimacy. The message had been crystal clear.

Then Fernando's voice made her jump. "Dreaming about your friend Carmela's wedding, Eviana?"

"Why not? She was so radiant with happiness that it would make anyone daydream about walking down the aisle."

Her reply had captured Ricardo's attention. Fernando stared at her, too, as though seeing her for the first time. "You're still a little young to be thinking of marriage," he told her.

"I don't think so," she informed him. "I've got some adult ideas on the subject."

"Such as?"

"Well, when the time comes, I don't want any old-fashioned nonsense. I think I have the right to live in the modern world and discard useless traditions. Time passes and the world changes, don't you agree?"

Eviana had chosen the wrong day to state her position on traditions. Fernando was gazing at her sternly. "What exactly does that mean?"

"That I'll marry the man I love, without bothering about other rules or standards," Eviana replied evenly.

Fernando might have been reading her mind, for it seemed that his next angry words were directed at Ricardo as well as Eviana. "Don't forget, young lady, that you're my ward until you turn twenty-one. I'll have a say in who you marry until then, and even afterward!"

Eviana didn't react to the threat as Lee expected her to. Instead of defending herself verbally, she shot her brother a look full of hatred and left the table.

ON A FINE, WARM December morning Lee strolled over to the corrals. From her bedroom window she had noticed Dominic and Julian Cartes counting the geldings, and she decided to walk over and watch them. As soon as he caught sight of her approaching, however, Julian found an excuse to move away. Irritated by his attitude, Lee decided to have it out with him then and there.

"Julian! I'd like to have a word with you," she called out. He stopped and turned anxious eyes toward her. "What have I done to make you avoid me this way?" she demanded.

Completely embarrassed, he stammered in a low voice, "Nothing, *señora*, believe me.... Excuse me, please, they're waiting for me in the stable." And he scurried away.

Dominic, who had witnessed the scene, refused to read any significance into it. "Why bother with Julian? I've already told you that he's eccentric with not much use for manners."

"Something like his daughter," Lee mused, suddenly remembering a brief encounter the two women had had near the linen closet the previous day. "It must run in the family. Each time Samantha sees me she looks the other way. This morning I passed her galloping away on Tampico, and she totally ignored me.... By the way, is she working as a linen maid or as a horsewoman? It seems every time I see her she's riding off somewhere."

Dominic shrugged. "Now that she isn't helping Rosa anymore she has more time to herself, I guess."

As Samantha's working hours weren't of much interest to Lee, she changed the subject. "Could you drive me to Dr. Chandler's office tomorrow morning, Dominic? I'd walk, but there's hardly any

shade on the road and I'm afraid of becoming faint."
And then there was the heaviness that had invaded
her limbs over the past few days....

Dominic agreed at once. "Of course, *señora*."

"Please, won't you just call be me by first name,
as you do Eviana and Fernando? After all, you're
practically one of the family."

Looking a little skeptical, he replied, "In Argentina we follow many customs. And I think that not
all the Valeras consider me like a relative.... What
time do you want to go to the doctor tomorrow?"

"Preferably after Fernando has left the house. I
don't want him to know about the visit until it's
over." A delicate fragrance rose to their nostrils as
she absentmindedly fingered several sprigs of jasmine that she'd plucked in passing.

"I'll come to the front door in the jeep around
nine o'clock," Dominic said.

She thanked him with a smile, then strolled over
to the cool shadow cast by the stable wall. Gazing
up at the crystalline blue sky, inhaling the perfume
of the jasmine, she had difficulty realizing that it
was winter elsewhere, and that a sharp wind was
probably blowing sheets of snow through the gray
streets of Boston.

Meanwhile, Fernando and Eviana had returned
simultaneously from their separate horseback
rides. Leaving her mount in the care of a groom,
Eviana ran to join Fernando, who just rounded the
corner of the tack shed. "We scarcely have the
chance to talk privately these days," she said. "I
want to discuss Samantha with you."

Slowly Fernando turned to face her, his expression set and belligerent.

A moment later, Lee turned the corner of the tack shed and overheard the angry exchange that made her blood run cold.

"It's stupid of you to leave Carioca tied up behind Samantha's house every morning where Lee can see him," Eviana was saying. "Everyone else may know what's going on but she doesn't...yet!"

Lee felt a sudden chill, despite the heat. Instinctively she flattened herself against the wall, longing to run away if she could just move her legs.

Fernando's voice retorted icily, "Keep your nose out of my personal life, Eviana."

"I just want you to be more considerate of your wife, especially now."

"Shut up! I forbid you—"

"You'll forbid me nothing, Fernando!" Eviana declared furiously. "I think it's despicable the way you're carrying on! Father would never have stood for it. And don't try to deceive me with lies. I'm not a child anymore. I know what's going on between you and Samantha."

Suddenly the anger left Fernando's voice. "Don't ever raise that subject with me again," he warned her. "You don't understand. Nobody could understand...."

It was a clear confession. Lee felt suddenly as if her whole world were collapsing around her. There was a loud buzzing in her ears and her vision became blurred. At that moment she had only one desire, to get back to the house without being seen and to lock herself in her room. But to do that she would have to go all the way around the stable and across the yard to the side door. With a tremendous effort she pushed herself away from the wall and took several tottering steps. Then the sky and the earth changed places, and Lee felt herself sinking into a silent void.

Chapter 10

"Help, someone, help!" Julian Cartes's cry brought everyone within earshot running, including Eviana and Fernando. As Julian explained how he had seen the *señora* stagger and then fall, Fernando knelt down beside his wife, calling her name. Eviana just stared in fright at her sister-in-law's pale face and colorless lips.

"We have to get her into the house," Fernando commanded.

Dominic stepped forward. "Let me do it," he said with authority. Gently he scooped Lee up in his arms and carried her toward the *casa*, Fernando and Eviana following closely behind.

As the strange procession came through the front door, Rosa wrung her hands in alarm. "What happened to the *señora*?"

"Go get something to waken her!" Eviana told her. "Quickly!"

Dominic set his burden down on the divan in the living room, and Rosa was at his elbow an instant later with a flask of vinegar and a wet cloth. But

despite all efforts to revive her, Lee remained
unconscious.

"We'd better get Dr. Chandler," Dominic said
then.

But Fernando shook his head. "Out of the question. Chandler isn't welcome here. Besides, she's
only fainted."

"We have to fetch Dr. Chandler at once,"
Dominic repeated firmly.

Fernando whirled to confront him. "You're in
charge of the stables, Dominic, and that's where
your authority ends. Stop trying to force your will
on this household!"

Not bothering to reply, Dominic turned to Rosa.
"Rosa, send for the doctor. I saw Ricardo beside the
garage. Tell him to take a jeep and drive into the
village right away."

Eviana voiced her agreement. "Dominic is right.
It's best to have a doctor here. Lee is pregnant and
this might be serious."

Pale with rage, Fernando yielded, but not without having the last word. "Go back to your horses,"
he told Dominic coldly. "You have nothing more to
do here."

Wordlessly Dominic left the room.

Lee had just opened her eyes when Dr. Chandler
arrived at Casa Rosàda. Immediately he sent the
Valeras out of the room so that he could be alone
with his patient. During the examination Fernando
paced the hall with growing agitation while Eviana
and Rosa waited silent and unmoving, near the
door of the living room. When Dr. Chandler finally
emerged, three pairs of eyes were fixed questioningly on him. But it was to Fernando that he said

frostily, "It seems your wife has suffered a terrible emotional shock."

"A shock?" Fernando sounded surprised.

"Yes. Her physical condition is rather unsteady right now," the doctor went on. "If she wants to keep this baby she's going to need plenty of rest and quiet. As a precaution, I want her to remain in bed for a few days, and she's to spend at least half of every day after that off her feet. You must see to it that she's kept calm. I'll stop in to check on her tomorrow." Then he nodded briefly to everyone and left.

The jeep that had brought him was waiting at the door, but with Dominic behind the wheel instead of Ricardo. "Get in, doctor, and I'll drive you home," he said. Once they were well clear of the ranch Dominic remarked, "Nothing serious, I hope?"

Dr. Chandler took a cigar out of his pocket and lighted it. "No. But she's going to have to take good care of herself."

Dissatisfied with the reply, Dominic insisted, "All the same, such prolonged unconsciousness isn't normal, is it?"

"Fainting isn't normal, period. You seem to be taking an unprecedented interest in my patient...."

"I like her and I feel sorry for her. You know why, don't you?"

Chandler sighed. "I'm afraid I do." Not another word was spoken until they reached the village.

STRETCHED OUT ON THE DEEP blue cushions of the divan, Lee was still pale when Fernando came into the room. He was struck by the bleakness of her expression and said anxiously, "You gave us quite a scare, *querida*."

Her eyes as they turned to meet his were filled with anguished resentment. "Let's drop the facade, shall we, Fernando?" she said in a weak, brittle voice. "I've had enough of your hypocrisy. I overheard you and Eviana talking out there. You and Samantha—"

"Lee, no!"

But she went on dully. "You've been betraying me, without a single thought for the child that I'm carrying." The brutality of her accusation seemed to rob Fernando of the power of speech. "Well? Say something!" she exhorted in a trembling voice. "Offer an excuse!"

Jaws clenched, hands balled into fists in his pockets, he remained stolidly silent.

"Tell me why you've made me a laughingstock, the butt of a bad joke," she insisted. "Did you think you could keep this from me forever?"

He turned and headed for the door.

"You're a spineless coward, Fernando!" she called after him, as he reached for the doorknob. He went rigid for a moment, then whirled around to face her.

"Forgive me," he said humbly. "If I have any excuse, it's that I knew Samantha long before I met you.... When I left for Europe, I'd just broken up with her. Far from home, I thought I could forget her. But as soon as we got back I realized it was impossible. That was why I wanted her out of the house, and why I suggested that we take a long tour of Argentina. But my struggles were in vain, because everything began again...."

Lee had thought that the moment she'd learned about Samantha had been the darkest of her life, but this muttered confession of infidelity was even worse. A wave of revulsion and despair washed through her, leaving her feeling even more weak and wretched.

"Try to understand, Lee," Fernando went on. "I'm not a monster...just an imperfect man. I have my faults, my—"

"Get out!" she told him in a voice that sliced through his apology like a knife. "If I were well enough, I would leave this house right now and never come back!"

"Lee, listen to me...."

"Get away from me! Leave!"

Alone once more, Lee gave in to the tears that she had refused to shed in the presence of her husband. Everything had come clear for her at last. How could she have been so blind? Everyone on the ranch had known—and all the villagers as well, she imagined—and not one of them had dared to tell her, not even Dominic.... Curiously, that was the part that hurt the most, for she had thought she'd finally managed to penetrate his facade of indifference and that a friendship was developing between them. She'd trusted him, but he had kept silent. She wanted very much to blame him for it, but found that she couldn't.

She began to remember details and events that had puzzled her at the time and to understand the meaning of the compassionate looks that she had sometimes received. She even understood Dominic's discretion. She realized, furthermore, why Fernando had made no effort to combine their two bedrooms, and why he'd taken no interest in their baby. And Julian Cartes had been avoiding her out of shame. The furor over the near-sale of Tampico, Samantha's too-frequent horseback rides, Fernando's inexplicable moodiness—suddenly Lee understood it all. Samantha had somehow repossessed her former lover. And the wife, honest and naive, had been the last to find out.

Lee's situation suddenly seemed hopeless to her. She was pregnant and alone in a foreign country. There was nobody she could turn to for comfort or for moral support. Any other woman might have called on her parents for sympathy, but Lee's family had been opposed to her marriage from the beginning, and she was afraid they might heap reproaches on her instead: "You were the one who insisted on marrying a man you'd known for only three weeks. You've made your bed, now lie on it...."

What would happen now? What about tomorrow? These were the questions that rose from the depths of Lee's disillusionment to overwhelm what little hope she had left. Dr. Chandler, after being made aware of what she had overheard in the yard earlier that day, had forbidden her to leave Casa Rosada. "You must rest," he had advised her. "Peace and quiet are absolutely necessary to your recovery from this shock. That is, if you really want to keep your baby." And she had suddenly realized that she had never wanted anything so much as she wanted to hold this baby in her arms.

That evening she locked the connecting door between her bedroom and Fernando's. It was an empty gesture, for he didn't try to see her. She didn't even hear him go to bed, although she laid awake for what felt like hours, finally crying herself to sleep after refusing the tray of food that Rosa had brought her.

Fernando left the house early the following morning for his daily ride, as if nothing had happened. Bitterly Lee realized that he had returned to Samantha's arms.

Dr. Chandler came back later and repeated his warnings, stressing the fact that the baby would be in danger if Lee didn't rest. So she kept to her room and Luisa brought all her meals up to her. Fernando stayed away, although Eviana made regular visits to her sister-in-law's room, probably, Lee thought numbly, for appearances' sake.

Toward the end of the week, most likely for the benefit of the *casa's* talkative staff, Fernando accompanied Eviana on one of her visits. But he didn't stay in his wife's room for long. "I'm glad you're feeling better," he said, as though reciting the phrases from memory, "and I hope that you'll soon be able to return to a less solitary way of life.... Forgive me, but I can't stay. I have to go to San Luis on business."

On business! Was he still hoping he could pull the wool over her eyes?

"You've been going into town a great deal lately," Eviana remarked.

"As often as necessary," he rejoined, declining to comment further.

Two days later, late in the afternoon, Luisa announced a surprise visitor—Dominic.

Lee felt her heart leap in her chest. "Dominic!" she echoed. "Send him in, Luisa." At last, a genuine, friendly visit, not an ordeal of small talk for the sake of appearances! Sitting up in bed she began to pat her hair into place. If only she'd thought to put on some lipstick after lunch. . . .

When Dominic entered the room he was carrying his hat in his hand as a mark of respect. "I hope you don't think I'm being presumptuous, *señora*," he began.

"Not at all, Dominic, Lee replied, smiling at him warmly. "I'm really glad to see you. And if you call me *señora* once more I'm going to scream!"

Suddenly he seemed to relax. Dropping his hat over the back of a chair, he sat down and said with unaccustomed warmth, "Rosa tells me you're improving. Is that true?"

She nodded. "Yes. I'm feeling much better."

"Then why aren't you outside enjoying this lovely spring day, instead of cooped up in a dark, stuffy room?" he demanded sternly.

"The heat—"

"At this hour of the day there's a cool breeze," he countered. "Come on, don't you even want to let in a little sunlight?" Before she could object, he went over to the windows, threw open the curtains and raised the sashes. Waves of golden sunlight and fresh, fragrant air flowed into the room.

"There," he said with a smile, "isn't that better?"

Lee nodded. *Fernando should have done that*, she thought miserably, fighting to swallow the knot in her throat. *He should have cared enough about me to stride in here and fling open the windows for my own good, whether I wanted them open or not. . . .*

Suddenly she was aware of Dominic's penetrating hazel eyes resting on her face, and she forced herself to smile as she looked up.

"Hasn't Dr. Chandler given you permission to go out yet?" he asked, sinking back into the chair.

"Yes, but I haven't wanted to." Even as she said the words, Lee knew that it was her own lack of courage keeping her indoors. The very thought of having to face all those curious stares, knowing what was running through the *peons'* minds as they watched to see what she would do next, was demoralizing. Lee herself wasn't sure what to do next.

As though reading her thoughts, Dominic leaned forward and said in a gentle voice, "Whatever has happened, and whatever is going to happen, you must be brave until the very end. An expectant mother sometimes finds she has incredible resources of strength, don't you agree...Lee?"

Touched to the quick, she felt tears burning her eyes. Whatever else he was, Dominic was her friend, probably the only one she had on the ranch. "You know that I...know now, don't you?" she stammered. "About Fernando and that woman?"

He nodded.

"I guess you've known about it for some time," she ventured uneasily.

Frowning, he got to his feet. "Going over all that can only cause more pain...."

Oh, please, don't go! "It's all right," she assured him anxiously. "I'm dealing with it."

But it wasn't to leave the room that he had gotten to his feet. Before she knew it he was half kneeling beside the bed, gazing earnestly into her face. "You mustn't let this embitter you," he advised her in a husky voice. "Everything can still be smoothed over between you and your husband."

"No, it can't, and...I don't want it to," she declared quietly. "My love for Fernando is dead." Her heart was pounding and there was a peculiar weakness in her limbs. Was it the pregnancy, or had she fallen once again under the spell of Dominic's hazel eyes? "I'm staying here just until the baby is born," she told him. "Then I'm leaving."

All at once the tension left his face. For just a moment Lee thought she glimpsed an ineffable sadness in his eyes, before their expression reverted to the grave mask she was so accustomed to seeing. "Then you must think of the baby," he said, getting smoothly to his feet again. He would have withdrawn, but Lee reached out and grasped one of his hands. "For the baby's sake you must get all the fresh air and sunshine you can," he continued, seeming to have difficulty following his train of thought. "You can't stay in this room...."

Suddenly he pulled his hand free and went to stand beside the chair, fingering the brim of his hat. "Forgive me, *señora*. I've taken impardonable liberties."

"No, wait," she protested, dismayed.

"I'd better go now."

"Dominic—"

At the door he stopped and looked back at her, and as their eyes met she saw the corners of his mouth turn up in a smile and felt her own lips responding. "I meant what I said about the fresh air and sunshine," he told her. Then he was gone.

Chapter 11

The following afternoon Lee went out into the garden. Relaxing on a chaise longue in the shade of a broad-leafed catalpa tree, she realized that she'd almost forgotten how delightful it was to watch the sun glinting off the plain and feel the warm spring breeze against her face.

About five o'clock, Rosa brought her a cup of *mate* and asked whether she would care to eat in the dining room that evening. After a moment's hesitation, Lee said yes.

When Fernando arrived late for dinner that evening and saw his wife in her usual place at the table, he declared with a forced smile, "I'm happy to see you among us again, *querida*." Lee suppressed a sigh. Hadn't he understood yet that it was futile to try to keep up appearances?

The meal was uneventful. Fernando hardly said a word, concentrating instead on drinking several glasses of wine. Lee noticed that his hands were shaking slightly.

Pleading fatigue, she was the first to leave the table, and she was stretched out on her bed when she heard Fernando enter his room a little while later. The door of his secretary creaked, then Lee heard the clinking of glass. He must have brought a bottle of liquor up to his room.

As she was dozing off, the knob of the connecting door began to rattle. Her heart was in her throat before she recalled that she had locked it.

"Open up, Lee!" Fernando said in a hoarse whisper.

She just lay there, holding her breath.

"Lee, open up! I have to talk to you!" Her persistent silence must have annoyed him, for he shook the doorknob furiously. "Unlock this door, do you hear me? You're still my wife!"

Lee listened, wide-eyed. His speech was slurred, and with a shudder of distaste, Lee realized that he had had too much to drink. How solid was that lock, she wondered. Could he break it open?

Once again he rattled the doorknob. "If you don't open this door I'll make a scene you'll never forget!"

She replied calmly, "Do whatever you like. Your behavior can't hurt me anymore."

In his rage, or perhaps out of clumsiness, he broke a glass and swore loudly. Then she heard him at the door again, cold and wrathful: "So this is your vengeance, is it? A locked door? Fine. Just don't hold your breath waiting for me to come knocking again!"

Lee bit her lip. He had just written the end to their married life together.

The following morning, she found a note that Fernando had slipped under her door before leaving that day. "Last night, among other things, I wanted to remind you that Alexia is coming to visit us today," he'd written. "To avoid embarrassment all around, I think it would be best not to let on that we're having problems. Fernando."

Lee suddenly remembered that Alexia had written to tell them she had accepted their invitation and was coming to Casa Rosada one day that week. But her misery of the past few days had banished all thought of the impending visit from her mind. Considering the cirumstances, she would have much preferred to put off meeting her husband's cousin. Dismally she realized that it was too late.

ABOUT TEN O'CLOCK THAT MORNING Alexia drove up to Casa Rosada in a sturdy station wagon. Fernando had returned from his morning ride early to greet her.

His cousin turned out to be an attractive young woman who seemed to radiate happiness and self-confidence. As they engaged in conversation, Lee's favorable first impressions were confirmed. Alexia was also endowed with boundless energy, uncommon good sense, perspicacity and tact. Lee was drawn to her right away.

Holding her newest cousin's hand, Alexia told her with a warm smile how absolutely delighted she was to meet her. And then she turned to Fernando and informed him, "You couldn't have chosen a more charming wife. And how good life has been to you, since there will soon be a baby in the house to cement your happiness."

Lee looked away, embarrassed, and Fernando said nothing. Alexia, sensing that her words had touched a nerve, didn't press the matter. Instead she turned toward Eviana and asked lightheartedly, "And what about you, Eviana? Do you have your eye on a young man?"

"I'm thinking about one," she replied with a smile.

Fernando made a sour face. "It's a long way from the thought to the reality," he pointed out.

"Speaking of reality," Alexia reminded him with a smile, "your sister isn't a child anymore. Some day soon a handsome young prince will come along and sweep her off her feet."

"If he's a full-blooded prince I'll raise no objections," Fernando remarked.

Alexia burst out laughing. "That was only a figure of speech! But when the time comes, you'll probably have very little to say about it. The qualities Eviana wants in a husband probably won't be all the same ones you'll be looking for in a brother-in-law."

Fernando looked dubious. "Why should they be different?"

"Because she'll be seeing with her heart and you'll be seeing with your head," Alexia explained.

Encouraged, Eviana chimed in, "I agree. One day I'll say to you, 'There's the man I want to marry.' And that will be that."

They had reached the living room. Fernando took up a position near one of the windows while the three women sat down on the divan.

"How are Jorge and the children?" Eviana asked.

Alexia apologized for her husband, who had stayed behind to mind the cannery. "He thinks he's indispensable, and I think he might be right," she confided with a smile. "As for the children, those little rascals are having a marvelous time running their grandmother ragged!"

In Alexia's bright company the morning passed very quickly. She had brought an atmosphere of relaxation and enthusiasm to Casa Rosada, and it made a refreshing change. Lee particularly appreciated her spontaneity and her kindness toward everyone she met. When Rosa came to serve refreshments, Alexia asked about her health and Luisa's. She also asked after Ricardo, in her estimation the best foreman in the district, and was eager to visit the stables and say hello to Dominic.

"He was such a good friend while we were growing up," she told Lee. "He's the one who taught me to ride."

As a favor to his cousin, Fernando suggested they invite Dominic to have lunch with them, an idea Alexia applauded. It was mainly thanks to her that the one-day truce continued to hold and the atmosphere remained friendly.

That afternoon Alexia, Eviana and Fernando visited Ramon's grave, while Lee returned to her chaise longue in the yard and Dominic went back to the stables. It was as they approached the *casa* again that Fernando suggested to the two women, "Why don't you two go back and spend some time with Lee? I have some business to attend to at the corrals."

Alexia gave him an inscrutable look. "I admire your dedication to the ranch," she said. "I wouldn't have believed you had it in you."

"You just don't know me, Alexia," he shot back cavalierly, and strolled over to the stables.

The two women continued toward the house. "Do you and Lee get along well?" Alexia asked suddenly.

"To tell you the truth, we hardly even talk civilly to one another," Eviana confessed.

"And is she the one who prefers it that way or is it you?"

Eviana sighed. "You know how I am. I'm a very private person, and once I form an opinion I tend to be very inflexible."

"I take it then that your hostility dates from Lee's arrival at Casa Rosada."

"It was so unexpected.... I just *knew* that Fernando's marriage had taken place too quickly. After all, he knew so little about her when he married her...."

"And you think she's an opportunist?" Alexia supplied.

"I think it's more likely that they married for convenience rather than for love. Consider the benefits to them both: Lee marries into money, and Fernando can bury the past and make father happy."

"I think you're wrong on both counts," Alexia said with a faint smile. "If Lee's only consideration were money, then she should be very happy, and she's not. She and Fernando aren't getting along at all." As Eviana stared at her in astonishment, Alexia went on, "Don't think I didn't notice how forced their smiles were. He's gone back to Samantha, hasn't he?"

"How did you know that?"

"What else could have caused such friction between newlyweds expecting a baby?" Alexia rejoined. "I had a feeling that his 'business' at the corrals was just an excuse."

"When Lee found out about it she collapsed with

shock and had to stay in bed for a week," Eviana told her glumly.

"One more bit of evidence that you're mistaken about her. A gold digger wouldn't have cared *who* he was sleeping with," Alexia remarked, then added with a sigh, "But how can Fernando carry on that way, knowing that his wife is expecting his baby?"

"It's mainly because of the baby that I condemn his behavior."

"And Lee has no right to your concern? Come, now, at the very least you have to admire her for her forbearance."

Eviana shook her head. "The only thing keeping her here is the pregnancy. After the baby is born, she'll probably leave."

"And if she did, all that would matter to you is the fact that a little Valera—one you already love— would grow up far from Casa Rosada, isn't that right? You're too miserly with your affection, Eviana! Don't you see that if you could overcome your indifference to her, Lee might not feel she had to leave here to be happy?"

Eviana smiled briefly. "Have you finished criticizing me?"

"Don't be angry. An older sister, if you'd had one, would have said the same thing."

"I'm not upset with you. Why don't you go on ahead? I'm going to have Rosa bring some coffee and, honey cake out to us in the garden."

While Eviana went to the kitchen in search of Rosa, Alexia rejoined Lee.

"It's good of you to keep me company," Lee told her. "I find this forced inactivity very hard to bear at times."

"This pregnancy is a trial for you, isn't it?" Alexia ventured.

"Yes, but also a tremendous joy."

Alexia wasn't surprised at Lee's reply. She knew from experience what a morale booster a pregnancy could be. As long as Lee could balance the promise of new life against her marital problems, she had a chance at happiness.

"Your joy hasn't begun yet," Alexia advised her with a smile. "Wait until you're holding that tiny, fragile person in your arms for the first time. A baby is totally dependent on you. It needs all your attention, but it will return your love tenfold."

Lee glanced sharply at her. Had Alexia spoken those last words by accident or by design?

"You can't imagine how impatient Eviana is to greet her new little niece or nephew," Alexia went on conversationally. "She adores children."

"Really?"

"Are you surprised?"

"A little, I must confess. She seems so...I'm sorry, but I was going to say 'cold.'"

"Seems is the right word, because it's only an appearance. It isn't easy to know Eviana. She's very deep. But she isn't cold, she's more...mercurial. A girl like that can be fire and ice. Eviana can be willful and jealous at times, but she's basically a good person at heart." Alexia paused for a moment, then went on. "My father used to refer to her as the savage of the family. And she's always reacted to strangers with a distrust. As a child she was like a wild fawn—you had to coax her and gentle her to gain her trust. That was one of the reasons Uncle Ramon sent her away to school instead of hiring tutors for her and keeping her on the ranch. And my own father had to force him to follow through on the decision, because Eviana didn't want to go and Uncle Ramon never could say no to her.... But Eviana has a good heart," Alexia repeated. "I hope that with time the two of you will learn to understand each other better."

Alexia left right after the honey cake and coffee, promising to return with her husband for the traditional *asado*, an open-pit barbecue to celebrate the New Year. Of course, this year's festival would be subdued because of the recent death in the family, but Ramon Valera's children knew they owed it to themselves to maintain the tradition anyway.

"Oh, and by the way, Lee," Alexia said through the open window of her station wagon, "Jorge and I would be delighted to have you over after the baby is born."

"Thank you for the invitation. May I confirm it closer to the time? Everything is so...up in the air right now...."

"We'll be counting on seeing you," Alexia insisted cheerily, and a moment later put the vehicle in gear and drove away.

Lee and Eviana waved to her from the front porch. Fernando still hadn't returned from his "business at the corrals."

Chapter 12

That evening Ricardo found Eviana waiting for him beside the garage when he pulled up in the jeep.

"Working overtime?" she asked with a smile.

He shook his head. "No. I met your cousin Alexia on the road and we pulled over and talked for a bit."

"About what?"

"Oh, just small talk. But it was pleasant."

"You see? You already have an ally in the family!" Ricardo laughed skeptically.

"By the way, Fernando and I had words today about marriage," she told him. "About you, although he didn't realize it...." Eviana repeated the conversation Alexia had started.

"And what does that change?" Ricardo asked, philosophically enough to be disconcerting.

"Now that I've planted the idea, I expect it'll be easier to talk to Fernando about us," she replied.

He leaned against the jeep and folded his arms across his chest "It's better to wait and see. You're still so young, Eviana...."

Her eyes were burning as she tilted her chin defiantly at him. "You keep saying that, but my mind was made up a long time ago. I want to be your wife, Ricardo!"

"Eviana..." he murmured tenderly, and cradled her small face in large, work-worn hands. Suddenly she found herself gathered up in a passionate embrace as he lowered his lips possessively over hers, but almost before she could respond he was pushing her away. A rueful expresssion had come over his features and she knew she would lose him to cold reason if they didn't act now.

"When do we talk to my brother?" she demanded.

"Is it that urgent?"

"Don't you love me, Ricardo? Or are you scared of my brother?" she cried.

"Be patient, Eviana! Ever since your father died I haven't had a minute to myself. Suddenly I have to do the work of two men. Lately I've even been digging in the fields alongside the *peons*. Let's wait until the growing season is over. And whatever you may think of your brother, he does have to be considered...."

Eviana sighed disappointedly. "Sooner or later you're going to have to face Fernando," she warned, and walked away from him, silhouetted by the golden light of sunset.

She arrived at the front door of the *casa* at the same moment as Fernando. He had seen her coming from the garage and he asked with a frown, "Where have you been?"

"Never mind me," she retorted angrily. "Where have *you* been?"

"In the west fields. I was with the *peons*."

"Ricardo just came from there, and he didn't mention seeing you."

Fernando refused to take the bait. "I was out with Hernandes's team.... What did you have to discuss with Ricardo that was so important you had to meet him at the garage?"

"Nothing." Then, perhaps because Ricardo's kiss had given her confidence or perhaps because she wanted to test the waters, she said suddenly, "What would you say if I chose to marry a man like Ricardo?"

Fernando said nothing, but fixed her with a gaze that was first incredulous, then angry. Eviana felt her self-assurance deflate immediately and, blushing fiercely, she raced upstairs to her room. It was not going to be easy, dealing with two such recalcitrant men, she thought wearily.

THE NEXT MORNING, shortly before it was time for Ricardo to leave for the fields, Fernando was riding Carioca in tight circles in front of the garage. As soon as he caught sight of Ricardo he summoned him with crisp authority, then wasted no time on amenities. "I've heard that you and my sister are secretly in love. I would like to believe that the report is false."

Despite the suddenness of the attack, Ricardo's features remained composed. "Who told you that?" he asked.

"Eviana, yesterday evening."

His face an impassive mask, Ricardo said evenly, "And have I made any declaration to you, *señor*, concerning your sister? Have you seen anything in my behavior that would indicate I was participating in such a relationship?"

Disconcerted by Ricardo's poised reply, Fernando still managed to retort, "Just be warned, Ricardo. Eviana is still a minor, and any romantic entanglement at this time would be out of the question for her. If I see the slightest evidence of a liaison between the two of you, I'll fire you on the spot." Seeing how unaffected Ricardo was by his threat, Fernando suddenly felt ridiculous. He shouldn't have taken his sister at her word. She'd only meant to provoke him. "It would be senseless, wouldn't it?" he added in a friendlier tone of voice.

Ricardo faced him down, a faint smile quirking the corners of his mouth. "I wouldn't know, *señor*. I haven't thought about it until now."

Fernando applied his spurs furiously to Carioca's flanks and set off at a gallop.

He was just approaching Samantha's house when he spotted the *padre* at the corner of the street. This was the last person Fernando wanted to meet. Fernando knew that according to custom he should have asked the priest out to the ranch. He would have issued the invitation, but he had suspected that the *padre* knew all about his infidelity and he had been afraid something would slip out in front of Lee. It had been a foolish precaution.

As Fernando was hitching Carioca's reins to an iron ring set in the fence post in front of Samantha's house, the *padre* came over to say hello.

"And how is Señor Valera?" he inquired with a smile. "I heard that she was quite ill and confined to her bed."

"She's much better, thank you."

"That's good to hear. When is the baby expected?"

"In June sometime."

"You are indeed a fortunate man, Señor Valera! How happy you must be! A small baby in a young household is always a blessing, isn't it?"

"Certainly," Fernando agreed uneasily.

Then, with perfect serenity, the priest added, "I wouldn't want to keep you, since you probably have many important things to do. I'll see you another time, *señor*. Give my best wishes to your wife."

Fernando waited until the priest had turned the corner before opening the gate to Samantha's house.

It seemed that he was destined that day to run across people he didn't want to meet. Leaving the village just before noon, he encountered Dr. Chandler behind the wheel of an ancient, temperamental Land Rover. The doctor was coming from the direction of the ranch. In a departure from custom that stunned Fernando, Chandler pulled his car over, got out and signaled to him to stop.

"I've just come back from seeing your wife," he told Fernando.

"What? Was it an emergency?"

"No. It was just a regular monthly checkup, and I can assure you that she's doing fine." As Fernando stared at him speechlessly, Chandler said a little testily, "Would you do me the courtesy of dismounting for a moment? I hate to look up while I'm talking. It makes me feel that I'm considered inferior to the person I'm addressing, and I happen to believe that I'm the equal of any man on this earth."

For a moment Fernando flared with anger. Who did this *peon* doctor think he was? He considered treating him with utter disdain and simply riding past him, but Fernando's curiosity got the better of him and he leaped to the ground instead, remarking testily, "Is that better, doctor? Has your complex disappeared?"

"Oh, I'm not the one with the complex," Chandler told him tranquilly. "And I won't keep you long. I just wanted you to know that on my way out of your wife's room I met your sister on the landing. In fact, she'd been waiting for me. She took me aside to insist that at the time of birth I relinquish the case to a specialist. I must tell you that I found her interference unwarranted, and I wondered if it was at your urging that she expressed that wish."

"No," Fernando told him coldly. "I'm sure my sister's behavior stems from her personal concern for the child about to be born into our family. She adores children."

"Nevertheless, your wife has asked *me* to deliver her baby, and I won't let her down. Naturally, I wouldn't hesitate to call in a specialist to *assist* at the birth should there be severe complications that might endanger the life of your wife or child. I just wanted to make that perfectly clear, and I would appreciate it if your sister would refrain from interfering in a matter that should be decided between my patient and myself. Agreed?"

Ordinarily, Fernando would have swept aside the presumptuousness of this man who had already humiliated the Valeras once. But under the circumstances he couldn't oppose Lee's wishes. "I wasn't the one who went to see you," he pointed out reluctantly, "but at the same time I won't hinder you from helping my wife. As far as I'm concerned, she's your patient. As for my sister, I doubt that she'll speak to you a second time about the matter."

The doctor smiled thinly. "That was what I wanted to hear." Then, as Carioca shook his splendid mane and pawed the ground impatiently, Chandler concluded, "I'll let you go now. *Hasta luego, señor!*"

Fernando arrogantly leaped into the saddle and galloped off.

It was just past noon when he arrived at the ranch. Leaving Carioca with a groom, he headed for the house, not noticing that Eviana and Ricardo were talking together at the far end of the yard.

"Your impulses can be very dangerous, Eviana," Ricardo was saying. "You'd better not talk to your brother any more about something you know he'll never agree to."

"You're more afraid of losing your job than of being separated from me, aren't you?" she accused him. "Be honest with me, once and for all, Ricardo!"

He raised a hand and caressed her cheek. "You have more courage than any woman I know," he said, smiling. "Hang on a while longer. Your twenty-first birthday isn't that far off."

It was practically a promise. Since Ricardo had asked her to, Eviana decided she would learn to wait.

OVER THE NEXT FEW WEEKS, things remained much the same at Casa Rosada. With the kindling of the

Argentinian summer, an air of expectation seemed to have settled over the countryside. Rows of long-leafed corn stalks loaded with swelling cobs striped the plain, while the wheat grew tall and golden for the harvest. And despite her emotional upheaval, Lee's physical condition gradually improved. Her pregnancy was following a normal course.

During this period, Alexia came back several times to visit her cousins. Twice she was accompanied by her husband, Jorge, a pleasant and reserved man who was still deeply in love with his wife. There was a tender understanding in the long looks and smiles they exchanged, and their children, attractive and engaging as they were, seemed to reinforce their parents' mutual affection.

The image of unblemished happiness they presented might have inspired a painful longing in Lee, but it also pointed up to her her many sources of consolation: Alexia's affection, Eviana's increasing warmth, Lee's own friendly relationships with Ricardo and Dominic, and especially the reality of the young life growing within her. Fernando, she knew, wasn't about to change. Coldly courteous in the presence of guests, he avoided her assiduously at other times. He had made no effort to reenter her bedroom, but Lee kept the connecting door locked anyway.

She knew that he spent most of his days either with Samantha at her cottage or riding Carioca around the ranch. Sometimes he drove in to San Luis for the day. She no longer watched him leave in the morning, nor did she care to notice the comings and goings of his paramour. Lee's despair at learning the truth had long since turned to weary acceptance.

The traditional *asado*, an open-pit barbecue to celebrate the New Year, took place in the huge front yard of the ranch. As usual, all the staff and their families were invited to the festivities. Samantha was the only person conspicuously absent.

The Valeras and their cousins oversaw the preparations for the *asado*. Lee watched in fascination as huge beef quarters and entire lamb carcasses were arranged on vertical spits, to be tended by several of the men. The women, meanwhile, served drinks, and soon the air filled with the music of the band assembled for the occasion.

Because they were still in mourning, the Valeras mingled only briefly with their employees, tasting the meat from the barbecue pit and wishing everyone a fine New Year. After that they returned to the house to dine alone. Out in the yard the local people continued to feast and celebrate in the tradition of the Argentinian *gauchos*, competing in games of riding skill. The summer night was warm, and the gentle breeze wafted the plaintive strains of guitar music to every corner of the ranch.

After the festival, life resumed its brisk pace. January and February ripened the crops for harvest. Jorge had purchased all the Valera corn to be processed at the cannery and exported. Of the wheat, soon nothing would be left but the stubble in the fields.

Because Lee found the afternoon heat too enervating, she made a point of taking a stroll each morning around the garden or else out to the corrals where she never tired of admiring the horses. Sometimes she even visited the *peons'* wives, who always made her feel welcome and didn't seem at all self-conscious about their modest hospitality. There was something special about relationships between women, Lee reflected, something marvelously egalitarian. Men were fence builders—it was they who had devised the rigid class structure of Argentinian society. But women tended to see fences as convenient leaning places while they talked to one another about their common concerns.

LEE AND EVIANA were first coming down for breakfast one morning when they heard the sound of cries and running footsteps outside. Straining to hear, Lee was surprised at the unusual commotion, but Eviana seemed unconcerned. "A stallion probably got out of the corral, and the men are trying to recapture him. . . ."

Suddenly the front door was flung open and Dominic raced into the vestibule. Pale and tense, he stopped abruptly, looking from one to the other of the two women who stood motionless at the foot of the stairs.

"There's been an accident," he said breathlessly.

Staring in anguish, Eviana blurted out, "Fernando?"

Dominic nodded. "He fell off his horse. They're bringing him in now."

Next they heard muffled voices, and four men appeared in the doorway, carring Fernando on a makeshift stretcher. Dominic directed them into the living room, where they deposited their charge on the divan then backed away in silence.

Dominic had to shake Rosa out of her terrified paralysis. "We need hot water and clean bandages!"

Eviana had knelt down beside her unconscious brother, while Lee leaned against the doorjamb, staring at his battered body. Fernando's clothes were torn and dirty. His face was badly bruised and scraped, and Lee saw that he had an ugly gash on his forehead.

Horrified, Eviana turned to Dominic. "We have to call Dr. Chandler!"

"I've already sent for him. He'll be here soon."

Then, gazing in bewilderment at Fernando's face, she stammered, "He—he isn't going to die, is he?"

Dominic helped her to her feet. "Dr. Chandler will take excellent care of him, don't worry."

"How did this happen?" she whispered.

"Nobody knows exactly.... Some workmen at the edge of a field not far from here saw a runaway horse dragging its rider by one foot. They managed to stop Carioca and release Fernando."

"Oh, Dominic, why didn't you dissuade Fernando from riding such a highly strung horse." Eviana cried.

"I warned him on several occasions, but he claimed he had Carioca under perfect control."

"And this is where it's led him," Eviana groaned as tears flowed unheeded down her cheeks.

Lee couldn't take her eyes off her husband's motionless body. Dominic noticed her then and must have realized that she was in a state of shock. Taking her gently by the shoulders, he said, "There's nothing you can do for him, *señora.* Luisa will help you up to your room. I'll keep you informed of any change in his condition."

Dr. Chandler arrived a few minutes later, along

with Ricardo, who led Eviana away. When Chandler had examined the patient carefully, he rolled up his sleeves and said, "He's in critical condition. He needs hospital facilities, but he's too badly injured to be moved. Otherwise I'd summon a rescue helicopter from San Luis. Compound fractures of the left leg and ankle, a crushed chest and massive head injuries.... His horse must have stepped on him a couple of times. I don't know whether I can pull him through, but we're sure as hell going to try."

"We?" Dominic echoed.

"You're going to assist me. Have Rosa bring a tub of hot water and some strong soap in here. We're going to have to scrub up first."

They struggled fiercely all through that day and the following night. Dr. Chandler performed major and minor surgery on the patient, and administered medications that had been rushed to the ranch within hours of his ordering them over the radio from the hospital in San Luis. But it was useless. Fernando died at dawn on the second day without ever regaining consciousness.

Dominic drove the exhausted doctor back to the village, then took his time about returning to the ranch. Looking for solitude, the foreman wandered into the tack shed. All manner of leather riding gear festooned the painted planks that passed for interior walls in the small, dirt-floored structure. The air was filled with the heady fragrance of well-used saddles, buts, and harness—not quite as pungent as the stables but just as pervasive. Wearily Dominic flicked the light switch by the door and sank into a straight-backed chair, peripherally noting the half-mended bridle on the tabletop to his right. As his eyes swept the room they halted automatically at the riding crop hung behind the door and his features gathered into a scowl.

Dominic himself had hung the riding crop there the previous afternoon. While Dr. Chandler stood vigil over his patient, Dominic had visited the scene of the accident. Splatters of Fernando's blood and torn fragments of his clothing had been strewn over the hundred-yard path that Carioca's wild dash had covered. The riding crop had been lying beside the trail, stained with blood, and he'd frowned at it for several moments before tucking it into his pocket. Now he stared at it again.

Impatiently he made as though to get up and snatch it from its hook, then abruptly changed his mind and settled back in his chair.

"No," he muttered to himself. "Let it be an accident. For her sake, let it be an accident...."

Chapter 13

A stuporous week followed the tragic accident that had claimed the life of Fernando Valera. For Lee, it was seven days spent floating between nightmare and reality before a sort of numbness settled over her.

Alexia had come to stay at the ranch to help out her distraught cousins, and she probably wouldn't have said anything if Lee hadn't told her quite candidly one day, "I don't want you to misunderstand, Alexia. I'm sorry he's dead, but I'm far from bereaved. I stopped loving Fernando a while ago. You know that he was unfaithful to me, don't you?"

Alexia nodded. "I know. That's why I'm sure that you'll be all right. We really shouldn't judge him, now that he's gone, but I think I can tell you something about him. I doubt, in a way, whether you ever really knew him.

"I told you when we first met that Eviana's character is very deep. It wasn't the same for her brother. In fact, at the time you met him, he was still very much under his father's thumb. He was searching for a way to assert himself, to become a man. Forgive me for raising the past, but he had just broken off with Samantha after an affair that had lasted for over a year. Uncle Ramon had opposed it from the beginning. One day, afraid that she might embarrass the whole family by managing to marry into it, he called Fernando into his office. After a stormy scene he'd browbeaten his son into breaking off with her and had convinced him to leave at once for Europe. In fact, his departure was a flight. He thought that, far from here, he could forget Samantha. Then he met you, fell in love, married you...."

"To stave off temptation," Lee murmured bitterly.

"No. I believe Fernando was genuinely in love with you. The death of his father and your hasty return to the ranch contributed to what happened later. As for Samantha, she must have been caught in her own trap and actually fallen in love with him. She must have schemed to get him back, refusing to give him up even though he was married."

But Lee had a different view of the facts. "It's also possible that Fernando regretted marrying me, after his father died and left him free to marry *her* if he wanted."

"That's groundless supposition, Lee."

"The fact remains that he went back to the woman."

"That's true," Alexia conceded. "But given time, after the birth of your baby, he might have overcome his weakness."

Lee shook her head. She had no illusions left, and

she knew that a home destroyed by a storm couldn't be rebuilt on the same spot. "He would never have been able to break free of her," she declared. "And in any case, it was too late."

"Then tell yourself that what's done is done, and look only to the future from now on."

"I've been doing that for a long while," Lee replied sadly.

GAZING LISTLESSLY OUT HER WINDOW, Eviana had seen Ricardo approach the house. Suddenly she remembered that this was payday for the field hands. He was coming to fetch the necessary money from the safe in her father's office. Breathlessly she raced down the stairs to meet him.

Ricardo was arranging bundles of bills in a leather briefcase when she came in. At the sound of the door opening he looked up, and without a word she threw herself into his arms and began to sob.

"Oh, Ricardo, I can't get him out of my mind. How could he have let himself be surprised by a horse he'd ridden for so many years?"

Gently Ricardo extricated himself from her embrace. "It was fate, Eviana."

"No, it was my fault! I wanted to be free so much that I could taste it. Now I'm cursing myself for bringing misfortune to my father and my brother."

"That doesn't make any sense. You know very well that a moment of bad luck is all it takes."

"No, I don't know that anymore," she sobbed. "I can't stand myself. Help me, Ricardo!"

He sighed with resignation as his face composed itself into a neutral mask. "You have nothing to feel guilty about, Eviana," he told her. "And it would be a waste of energy anyhow, because your plans will never work out. Please forgive me for hurting you like this, but I won't marry you, Eviana. We'd never be happy together because I don't love you. I like you very much, but I don't love you."

"It isn't true," she whispered in horror. "It isn't possible...."

"Please, give up this impossible idea. We'll never marry."

"Why did you lead me on, let me believe that you...?" she demanded, bewildered.

"I tried a hundred times to make you see reality, but you refused."

Her eyes fixed on Ricardo's face, she murmured, "Reality. It's another woman, isn't it?"

"No."

Abandoning all her pride, she pleaded, "Ricardo, you have to tell me the truth. Don't just drop me like this. You're hiding something, I can feel it. Why reject me now, just when I thought I had the right to think—"

"You were deluding yourself."

"Deluding myself?" When you held me so tenderly in your arms and asked me to be patient?"

"It was wrong of me. I should never have said that."

She stared beseechingly at his stubborn, impenetrable face for a moment, then raced blindly up to her room and flung herself down on the bed.

Moments later there was a gentle knock at the door and Alexia came in. Her lips tightened momentarily at the sight of the pale, disheveled girl on the bed. "Darling," she said sitting down on the edge of the mattress, "I know you loved him very much, in spite of your differences. And it's natural to grieve over his death. But when I see you teetering on the edge of depression, not sleeping, not eating.... I'm scared to go home and leave you. I've decided to send for Dr. Chandler. Perhaps he can prescribe something for you."

Eviana sighed. "I don't care," she muttered wearily.

Thinking that he'd been summoned to Casa Rosada because of Lee, Chandler came at once. As soon as Rosa had shown him into the living room where Alexia was waiting, he inquired after his patient.

"Lee is doing fine. It's Eviana I'm worried about. I'm afraid she's headed for a breakdown," Alexia told him. "You must see her, doctor."

"Did you tell her I was coming?"

"Yes. She's waiting for you."

Eviana emerged from her lethargy just once, to remark ironically, "So you have a few minutes for me today, doctor?"

Ignoring the barb, he took her pulse rate. The last time he had seen her she had been proud, scornful and erect. But now she was just a frail girl with a taut and desperate face, and eyes that blinked more often than necessary.

A thorough examination confirmed that there was nothing physically wrong with her. The problem was entirely emotional. All rancor gone, he told her kindly, "I'm going to try to help you, but you have to work at it, too. I know how hard it is to lose someone you love. But life goes on and so must we."

"I'd like to go to sleep and never wake up again," Eviana said bleakly.

"It's a sin for someone your age to be talking about suicide!" he snapped. "You have your whole life ahead of you. And even though you may not think so right now, you *will* be happy again." Dr. Chandler patted her hand comfortingly. "If my words don't do anything for you, maybe my prescription will."

His prescription, which he gave to Alexia, consisted of medication, which Alexia herself was to administer to Eviana. "She has to relax, and quickly," the doctor warned. "A change of surroundings would help. Could she get away from here for a while?"

Alexia didn't hesitate for a moment. "I can take her home with me."

"That's a start. She needs to be distracted from herself."

"Well, she loves children, and I have three who are bound to keep her busy," Alexia said with a smile.

"Excellent!"

Once the doctor had left, Alexia went to inform Eviana of the plans that had been made. But Eviana was lying on her bed, apparently asleep, and Alexia withdrew silently.

The next day, silent and distant, Eviana helped Rosa and Alexia to pack her bags. They left late in the afternoon, when the heat had abated. Ricardo was nowhere in sight.

When the gardener had loaded their bags into the trunk of Alexia's car, Eviana turned to Lee and said, "You're the mistress of Casa Rosada now. Did you foresee that?"

Gazing at the thin, angry face, Lee felt a wave of pity. Brushing aside the question, she corrected her, "I'm only the temporary guardian of Casa Rosada. Until you get back, Dominic and Ricardo will continue to run the ranch, as they've been doing since your father's death."

Then Eviana got into the car. Alexia kissed Lee and advised her, "Take care of that baby, and be sure to keep us posted. And don't hesitate to call me if you need me!"

Rosa stood behind her in the tiled corridor, wiping away tears, as Lee's eyes followed the car that became smaller and smaller in the distance until finally the fields swallowed it up.

WITH EVIANA GONE, Lee found the house lonely. Still, she loved Casa Rosada. She had become attached to its picturesque setting, and to the familiar sounds that surrounded it—the slow grating of the windmill in a breeze, the distant whinnying of horses and the strumming of a *peon's* guitar at the end of a long afternoon. Rosa and Luisa bustled around during the day, however, and in the evening there were Dominic and Ricardo, still attending the evening meal.

Out of habit, or perhaps respect, the two foremen began reporting to Lee at the dinner table, just as they'd done with Ramon and then Fernando. Ricardo talked about the harvest and all the preparations that would have to be made for it. Dominic reported on the stud farm. Both of them looked ahead to possible future sales of grains and horses.

"Please don't feel you must keep me abreast of business matters," Lee told them one evening. "I really don't have any rights on the ranch, or on this house."

Dominic glanced sharply at her. "But your child will," he reminded her.

"For the time being, Eviana is the owner of the property," Lee insisted.

In her sister-in-law's absence, Lee made only one management decision. Several days after Eviana had left, Lee told the foremen she wanted to settle a situation that had become intolerable to her. "It's Samantha Cartes," she explained. "While I'm living in this house I don't want to have to set eyes on her again. We can dismiss her and hire another linen maid. Would one of you please inform her of that, and tell her also that I'll continue to pay her wages until she finds other work?"

"You see old Julian every day," Ricardo said to Dominic. "Maybe you'd better talk to him."

After a moment's reflection, Dominic agreed.

"Thank you. I realize it's a rather ticklish job," Lee went on. "I feel sorry for Julian. I hope he'll understand that I'm not being spiteful. I just want to forget about Fernando's...indiscretion."

Lee was quite willing to pay to be rid of Samantha. When they had returned from Europe, Fernando had given his wife a generous monthly allowance. But Lee was accustomed to living quite modestly and had hardly touched the money. Well, now she had a use for it, she mused. She certainly wouldn't be taking any of it back to the States with her.

THE CORN HAD BEEN HARVESTED, the flowers in the garden had withered and the leaves of the catalpas were dry and yellow when Eviana returned to Casa Rosada. Autumn had faded the grandeur of the immense plain and filled the skies with swirling gray clouds.

Dr. Chandler's treatment and the love of Alexia and her family had brought Eviana through her emotional crisis. But the wound Ricardo had inflicted had still not healed. The very sight of him aroused painful memories, although Eviana was able to maintain her outward calm. And she was imbued with a determination that Lee and the others were soon to hear about.

Six weeks had gone by, as confirmed by the rounded belly under Lee's black dress. Black suited her—it pointed up her fair coloring. For the first time, Eviana found that it was comforting to have her sister-in-law in the house. "I'm glad you're here," the younger woman said with utter sincerity.

Lee smiled at her. "I'm glad you're back. We've all missed you."

It was at their first dinner together that Eviana suddenly put down her fork and declared, "I have something important to tell you. While I was at Alexia's I had a great deal of time to think about Fernando's strange accident." She paused to let her first word sink in. Then slowly, she said, "I've come to the conclusion that it wasn't an accident—he was too good a horseman.... I think he was murdered."

Chapter 14

Lee and Ricardo stared at each other, dumbfounded.

"And how did you arrive at that conclusion?" Dominic asked.

"The day after the accident I visited Carioca in his stall. He was still nervous and upset, and I noticed a cut on his neck. Didn't you see it?"

"It never occurred to me to examine the horse," Dominic replied with some hesitation.

"At the time I didn't attach any importance to the detail. But later it dawned on me that that wound couldn't have been made by a riding crop. Besides, Fernando would never have abused a horse that way."

"Neither Julian nor the groom who took care of Carioca noticed any wound," Dominic said in puzzlement. "They would have mentioned it to me. Are you sure it was Carioca you were looking at?"

"Of course!" Eviana declared impatiently. "The cut has probably healed by now, but six weeks ago it was quite obvious. I'm not mistaken, Dominic." He shrugged fatalistically. "What's more, I visited the stables this afternoon. And behind the tack shed door I found Fernando's riding crop. It had bloodstains on it."

Ricardo frowned. "I'm afraid I don't see the significance of that."

"Don't you realize that someone had to bring the riding crop back from the scene of the accident?" Eviana cried. "Carioca's groom didn't do it. In fact, nobody that I've spoken to could even recall seeing it that day, and yet we all know that Fernando never went riding without it. It was a status symbol for him."

Glancing across the table, Lee noticed a pecularly hard expression in Dominic's eyes.

"But that's not what's important," Eviana went on excitedly. "The critical thing is that there isn't any explanation for the wound on Carioca's neck *or* the blood on Fernando's riding crop. I felt that these two details bore looking into, so I've sent a special delivery letter to the magistrate's office, requesting an investigation."

Dominic broke the astonished silence to object, "But all you have are suspicions. Don't you think it would have been better to talk to us about it first?"

"There was no point. You know as well as I do that my brother was too good a rider to be unseated by any unexpected move from a horse. And there was no apparent reason for Carioca to bolt."

"But you know how highly strung Carioca is," Lee argued. "I'm pretty sure myself that the horse alone was to blame."

Eviana stood her ground. "I'm not going to be sure of anything until the results of the investigation are in."

"Why would anyone attack your brother?" Ricardo demanded.

"Jealousy, hatred..." Eviana replied shortly. "I'm sure he had enemies. One of them could have been lying in wait for him out there."

"I was one of his enemies," Lee pointed out softly.

"I'm not making any accusations," Eviana assured her. "I only want to clear up the mystery. It might be a simple matter for a trained investigator to determine what happened. If so, we'd be fools to live with the uncertainty."

Ricardo had already begun eliminating suspects. "I don't see who could have taken your brother's life. The stable crew and field hands had only a nodding acquaintance with him. The staff of the *casa* couldn't have done it. Fernando never even spoke to the villagers. Forgive me for mentioning this, *señora*," he said to Lee, "but the only house he ever visited there was Samantha's...."

"Exactly!" Eviana crowed. "Julian might have wanted revenge because Fernando didn't marry his daughter."

"That's ridiculous!" Dominic exclaimed. "I know Julian better than anyone, and if Fernando and Samantha's behaviour inspired any emotion in him, it was shame. Besides, it would be easy to prove that he was working around the corrals at the time of the accident."

"Then someone else may not have such a good alibi," Eviana told him evenly.

"You mean me, and Dominic?" Ricardo demanded incredulously.

"Possibly."

Ricardo frowned. "Are you implying...?"

"I'm not implying a thing," Eviana cut him off. I'm only saying that you'll be questioned along with everyone else on the ranch when the magistrate's investigators arrive."

"It's been six weeks," Lee pointed out. "How do you know they'll bother?"

"For a Valera, they'll bother," Eviana declared flatly.

Dominic left the table early that evening. Before returning to his bungalow he paid a visit to the tack shed. The riding crop was gone.

TWO DAYS LATER, in midmorning, the special investigators appointed by the district chief of police arrived by car. Before driving out to the ranch, they had stopped in the village to secure accommodation and to discuss the price of meals with the owner of the cafe, who had himself agreed to put them up since there was no hotel or rooming house.

Inspector Otijo, who seemed to be about thirty-five, was in charge of the investigation. His assistant was a young officer named Garcia.

"The rooms at the cafe will be quite simple," Eviana told Otijo. "If you'd prefer to stay in one of our bungalows—"

He wouldn't let her continue. "It's better if we stay in the village and mingle with the people who frequent the cafe. One of them might let something slip in conversation that would be valuable to our case. You know, we don't have much to go on in this investigation. It's a shame you didn't call on us at the time of the accident."

The two officers were as different from each other as day and night. Otijo was a large, calm man who gave the impression of having great physical strength. He had thick black hair and a stubborn face, and always seemed to be watching for something through his narrowed eyes. Garcia, on the other hand, had an almost absentminded air about him. His colorless eyes looked sleepily out at the world through a thick pair of horn-rimmed glasses.

Eviana took them into her father's office and answered their questions for more than an hour, providing facts and details, which they jotted down scrupulously in small black notebooks. Then she opened a desk drawer and produced the riding crop, which was wrapped in a clean cloth. She told them where she'd found it and showed them the dried blood. "I don't know who brought it back," she said, "but the *peons* who helped my brother all swear he wasn't holding it in his hand after the accident."

"Are you sure he took it with him that day?" Garcia asked.

"Absolutely. He never went riding without it."

"It was very intelligent of you to preserve any possible fingerprints," Otijo observed. "We'll send it to the forensic lab right away."

That afternoon they asked to be shown the scene of the accident. But more than six weeks had elapsed since Fernando's death, and despite their painstaking examination of the site, they didn't turn up anything of significance. Once again, thanks to the *peons*, they were able to determine approximately where Fernando had fallen off his horse.

Afterward they visited the stable and asked to

see Carioca. Although the stallion's neck bore a
barely visible scar, there was no way of determin-
ing when the wound had been inflicted or with
what kind of instrument.

When the officers returned to the *casa*, Eviana
introduced them to Lee, warning them not to tire
her out with too many questions. "She doesn't
know any more than I do," she added. "Probably
less. We were about to have breakfast together
when they brought Fernando into the house."

Nodding, Otijo assured her that he would be
brief as possible. It wasn't necessary to explain the
unpleasant marital situation, since Eviana had
already done that, not wanting to hide anything
about her brother.

"Do you know of anyone who hated your husband?" Otijo asked.

"Not among our staff."

"And in the village?"

"No, I think Eviana's imagination is behind all
this business of a murder."

"That's precisely what we're here to decide,
señora.... Forgive me for being indiscreet, but did
you and your husband ever argue about his meet-
ings with Samantha Cartes?"

"I wouldn't call our one confrontation an argument," Lee said slowly.

Garcia was standing off to the side, as still as a
statue, but studying Lee's face closely.

When they had finished with her, they pro-
ceeded to question Rosa, Luisa and all the other
servants in the house. Then, at nightfall, they
waited to speak to Ricardo and Dominic. Garcia had
already compiled quite a list of facts about both of

them from the information given by the others.

Ricardo told them that at the time of the accident he had been in the fields with a team of laborers. "I only left them for about fifteen minutes, to check on some other workers in the next field."

"And how did you go?" Otijo asked.

"In the jeep."

"Did you get along well with Señor Valera?" Otijo asked.

"We had no reason not to get along. Señor Valera was always satisfied with my work."

Garcia started, as though awakening suddenly from a light sleep, and insisted, "No reason at all to quarrel?"

"I told you, no," Ricardo repeated impatiently.

"And yet we understand that you two argued about his sister not long ago."

"We exchanged words," Ricardo said with a shrug.

"Why was that?"

"He thought I was having an affair with his sister. Nothing could have been farther from the truth, as Eviana herself can tell you."

"Very well," Inspector Otijo remarked, taking over the questioning again. "Now, can you think of anyone who might have wanted to harm Señor Valera?"

"No. I can tell you that he wasn't universally loved. But I don't think that proves that anyone necessarily wanted to murder him."

When Ricardo was released, it was Dominic's turn to be questioned. Before the officers had even asked, he gave them his full name and the nature of his work at Casa Rosada and then declared, "I may as well tell you that I have no alibi for the time of the accident."

Inspector Otijo asked in an even voice, "And where were you at that time, Señor Fontanera?"

"I was riding a horse out in the fields."

"Well, well!"

"I do that sometimes, when I'm not busy. And I had about half an hour free that morning."

"Did you ride through the village?"

"You mean did anyone see me and can they corroborate my story? Not that I know of."

"Were you on good terms with Señor Valera?"

"You probably know that I grew up in this house. Consequently I feel a certain affection for the Valera family. That never prevented Fernando and me from disagreeing at times, however. Our personalities were radically different and I didn't approve of his conduct. But that doesn't mean that I wanted him dead."

"What does Eviana Valera mean to you?"

"Something less than a relative, but much more than a stranger. A sort of foster sister, if you like, although I doubt that she ever thought of me as a foster brother."

"Do you get along well with Señora Valera?"

"Lee Valera and I are practically compatriots. We get along excellently."

His hands clasped behind his beefy back, Otijo took several steps across the room, then returned to plant himself in front of the foreman.

"You realize, don't you, that your lack of an alibi is very damaging?"

"Yes, but I'm not about to make one up just to appease your sense of order."

"This isn't a joking matter. You could be in serious trouble...unless you overheard or saw something while you were out riding?"

"If I had, I would have told you."

"Were you near the scene of the accident?"

"No, I was at the opposite end of the property. I rode south that morning."

"Thank you," Otijo said, ending the interview. "I would just ask you to remain available for further questioning if necessary."

The next day, at the stable, it was Julian Carte's turn to submit to an interrogation. He proved easily that he hadn't left the corrals that fatal morning, but the officers kept at him for a long time, until he finally broke down and confessed how ashamed and angry Samantha's affair with Fernando Valera had made him feel. Then, just as he thought it was all over, Otijo unsheathed his claws again.

"Did it ever occur to you to plot against Señor Valera? To make him have an 'accident?'"

"Plot?" the astonished man echoed.

"You might, for example, have given his horse a drug that would make the animal bolt or behave wildly."

Cartes drew himself up indignantly. "I find your accusation most insulting!"

Otijo shrugged and gestured appeasingly with his hand. "It was just a supposition."

"The only drugs we have here are medications prescribed by Dr. Chandler for the horses, and it's Señor Fontanera who administers them," Julian said angrily. "There they are, on those shelves." And he pointed at a sort of medicine chest behind Garcia, which contained ointments, syrups and several flasks with hand-written prescription labels.

Otijo nodded to his assistant. "Gather them all up for the lab," he ordered. When that was done he turned back toward Julian Cartes and said, "We'll be back to talk to you again. *Hasta luego.*"

The next visit they paid was to Dr. Chandler. He, too, had to give his full name and a brief history of his life, including the reason he was practising medicine in this tiny village. Without hesitation, he explained that none of the medications at the ranch could possibly cause dangerous excitation to a horse and added, "Chemical analysis will confirm what I say. But, if a drug *was* administered somehow, and if there were still some of it left, I doubt that the culprit would have been stupid enough to leave it lying around."

"Then you state categorically that you never furnished any dangerous drugs to Dominic Fontanera?" Otijo repeated thoughtfully.

"Absolutely."

"They say in the village that you and he are friends."

"I suppose we are. Why?"

"This is an official police investigation, Dr. Chandler," Otijo reminded him sternly. "We have to get all the facts. I also happen to know that you don't like the Valeras very much."

Chandler smiled ironically. "I'm not very fond of Ramon Valera's children, that's true. But I've always liked Lee."

"Because she's an American, like yourself?"

"That's part of it, I guess."

"Apparently, however, you intensely disliked Fernando Valera."

"At times. At other times he just got on my nerves a little. But there's a wide gulf between disliking someone and wishing him dead," Chandler pointed out dryly.

From his corner near the door, Garcia said suddenly, "For the moment, nothing indicates that you're implicated in this affair, doctor." Then the two officers left.

They spent the rest of the morning at the cafe. The evening before, they had made a point of getting to know the regular patrons of the place, and they'd spent a long time drinking warm bitter beer with the village men in an attempt to cull any information that might help them clear up the Valera affair.

That afternoon they went to Samantha's cottage.

The villagers had told them about a pretty, exuberant and rather haughty girl with velvety eyes and a shapely figure. What they found instead was a distraught woman with tragic features, her hair and clothing disheveled, her home in disarray. She showed them into her tiny, cluttered living room, and when Inspector Otijo explained why they were there, she nodded dully.

"I know. My neighbor told me about it.... You've come to question me, but I can't tell you anything. That morning I was waiting for Fernando, as usual. He didn't come. Later I found out from the villagers that he was dead." She choked back a sob.

"You loved him?" Garcia asked.

"As much as he loved me. Nothing could have kept us apart," she said, her eyes filling with tears. "Nothing but death!"

"And how do you feel about his death?" the officer asked.

"That it's unfair! To die so young, of such a commonplace accident...it's horrible."

"His family believe he was murdered. You don't agree?"

Her eyes widened slightly as she replied, "No. I think the truth is simple and senseless."

"When you realized he was late that day, didn't you make any effort to go and meet him?" Garcia wanted to know.

She shrugged. "I couldn't. He didn't always take the same route. So I just kept waiting and watching from my window. Manuela, my neighbor, saw me. She was washing clothes outside."

Suddenly Garcia was at Samantha's elbow. "I suppose you know Dominic Fontanera?"

"Yes," she replied warily.

"What do you think of him?"

Samantha seemed stunned. "I don't see what that has to do—"

"Just answer the question."

"He's a good man," she told him defiantly. "Everyone likes him. My father works under him and has never had occasion to complain."

"Did Fernando Valera ever intimate to you that he had quarreled with Fontanera?"

"Never."

"And how about with your friend Orlando Hernandes?" Garcia asked calmly.

Samantha's eyes flashed. "Go ask him yourself!" she snapped.

Garcia glanced at his partner. Otijo was shaking his head.

"Thank you, Señorita Cartes," Otijo said gently, urging the younger officer toward the door. Once outside he reproved him, "You mustn't press so hard. We're here to uncover the facts, not prosecute the case."

"That girl knows a lot more than she's telling!" Garcia declared hotly. "Didn't you see the look in her eyes when I mentioned that Valera might have been murdered?"

Otijo chuckled softly to himself. "They're all holding back on us, my eager young friend. Let's just wait a bit and see whose secrets are relevant to the investigation. Then we'll close in like wolves to the kill...."

Chapter 15

Several days passed, during which the two police officers worked tirelessly to throw some light on the death of Eviana's brother. They had become well acquainted with the life and problems of the victim and his associates. Their investigation had been painstakingly methodical, as they gleaned every possible fact from the many interviews and conversations they had held. They had reconstructed in minutest detail the life of Fernando Valera, from the day he had returned to the ranch to the day he died.

Although the lab hadn't been able to find anything incriminating among the medications they had seized at the stables, Otijo and his assistant were convinced that Eviana was right. Someone had arranged Fernando's accident. Forensic examination had revealed that the blood on the riding crop was Fernando's, and—this detail alone was important and disturbing—the only fingerprints on the instrument belonged to Dominic, who had admitted to finding it on the path and bringing it back to the tack shed.

Everything seemed to point to the foreman, especially since he hadn't been able to furnish an alibi. However, the police officers had still to discover the motive for the crime.

The two men had returned alone one morning to the scene of the accident and had reexamined the ground inch by inch, from the spot where the victim had fallen to the place where the *peons* had stopped the horse. After more than an hour of careful inspection, they finally uncovered an old, bent shovel, eaten with rust and bearing brown traces that they speculated might be dried blood. It had been concealed beneath a spiny bush and so had escaped notice on first and even subsequent inspections. Analysis revealed that the brown traces were, in fact, dried horse blood. The policemen surmised that the cutting edge of the shovel might have struck Carioca on the neck, causing him to bolt in fright. But unfortunately, the handle of the shovel was clean of fingerprints.

Otijo decided to question Eviana, Lee and the two foremen again. Eviana couldn't tell them anything new. As for Ricardo's alibi, it was easily established that even in a jeep, he couldn't possibly have crossed the entire width of the ranch, committed the crime and returned to his men in so short a time.

"So you see, I'm innocent," Ricardo said.

"Unless you had hired an accomplice," Garcia put in casually.

"You mean a hit man?" Ricardo scoffed. "And what would my motive have been? I don't covet Fernando Valera's sister *or* his money, and I had no grudge against him."

"His widow is a very pretty woman," Garcia pointed out.

A fleeting shadow crossed Ricardo's face. "So?"

"Do you think Lee Valera will remarry?" Otijo interjected."

"I don't know. It's possible," Ricardo replied.

"Will she find a worthy suitor in this district?"

"Worthy or not, she'll have as many as she wants."

"Obviously, she's quite a catch," Garcia murmured. "She's beautiful, rich, intelligent.... Do you suppose you and Dominic Fontanera might try your luck with her?"

Ricardo shrugged nervously. "Not me...but Dominic might. He's been smitten for some time." As soon as the words were out of his mouth he realized that he'd given Dominic a motive for wanting Fernando out of the way. Then he reminded himself that all he had done was tell the truth, after all....

"Are you sure of that?" Otijo demanded.

Ricardo, who knew Dominic very well, couldn't deny it. "I'm sure," he said gruffly.

When Ricardo had gone the two officers compared notes.

"It's a perfect motive for murder," Garcia remarked. Señora Valera is a beautiful woman married to an unworthy man. Why not kill the hated rival?"

"That's true," Otijo admitted. "But there's something about this that doesn't sit well with me. The net is tightening around Fontanera a little too readily. Everything points to him, it's too perfect. And if I were going to dispose of someone, I'd make sure I had an unshakeable alibi, wouldn't you?"

"Yes, if I were *planning* to commit a crime. But what if it happened spontaneously, in a burst of rage, for example? One man hits another during an argument, the second man falls and strikes his head and dies. And there are clues and fingerprints all over the place."

"And if those clues and fingerprints are still there six weeks later, we must conclude that our suspect is either incredibly stupid or incredibly arrogant...or innocent," Otijo pointed out quietly. "The riding crop hung in the tack shed for over a month. Fontanera had plenty of opportunity to wipe his fingerprints off it, yet he neglected to do so. Why?"

Garcia shrugged. "I don't know. I do know, however, that we have a prime suspect, with both motive and opportunity, and at least one piece of incriminating evidence. If we don't lay a charge, our superiors are going to want to know why."

Pursing his lips, Otijo began drumming his fingers on Ramon Valera's polished desk top. "I still don't like it," he said.

"I haven't liked it from the beginning," Garcia pointed out. "It was a stale case when they handed it to us, and we've had to scrounge for every clue. We've taken this investigation as far as we can. You know we have, and you know we have enough against Fontanera to lay a charge. We're here to gather facts, remember? Not to judge."

"All right," Otijo sighed. "Let's get this over with."

Dominic had finished lunch and was about to return to the corrals when the two officers knocked at the door of his bungalow. They showed surprise at seeing the pleasant and tidy apartment he occupied in the outbuilding just to the west of the main house.

"Can I offer you something, *señores*?" Dominic suggested guardedly.

"No, thanks."

"Then may I know what brings you here?"

"Just a few questions," Otijo replied laconically.

And thus began another grueling interrogation, which soon had Dominic's nerves on edge. Questions and answers were volleyed back and forth for half an hour before Otijo broached the crucial point: "How did you feel about Fernando Valera's treatment of his wife?"

"I thought it was despicable," Dominic replied frankly. "She deserved better than that."

"Did you ever tell Señor Valera how you felt?"

"No, he never would have tolerated my—Wait a minute. Why are we going over these details?"

"Because they're important. You've said that you thought he was despicable. Why? Because he was unfaithful to his pregnant wife?"

"Yes, I suppose."

"Or was it mainly because you loved her?"

Dominic started violently. "You have no right to ask that," he stated vehemently.

"Oh, but we do, Señor Fontanera. We now have proof that Fernando Valera was murdered. You have no alibi and you have an excellent motive for committing the crime. You love Lee Valera—probably you were attracted to her from the first day she arrived here. Seeing her so unhappy, especially when she found out she was being betrayed by her husband, was more than you could bear.

You began to hate the man who was making her suffer, and you decided to do away with him!"

Dominic looked from one unsmiling face to the other incredulously. "You're crazy, both of you!"

Then Garcia's lazy voice cut in. "Don't get so excited, *señor*. It'll go easier for you if you make a full confession right now."

"Confess what? That the inanities pouring out of your imagination have any basis in fact?" Dominic exclaimed, beside himself. "What evidence do you *really* have against me?"

"Several strange coincidences that you're going to have to explain in front of a magistrate, *señor*," Otijo said gravely.

"Such as?"

"You were riding a horse in the countryside at the moment of the incident. You claim to have been at the opposite end of the property from Señor Valera, but we have only your word on that. You also admitted having picked up the riding crop at the scene of the crime—"

"Several hours later!"

"It has only your fingerprints on it."

"Of course it does! If I were guilty of a murder, do you really think I would have left them there? And do you think I would have brought the riding crop back to the tack shed myself?"

"I'm sorry, but you're going to have to come to San Luis with us for further questioning," Otijo told him.

Dominic's hands balled into fists. "You have no right—"

"This warrant gives us the right," Garcia explained, reaching into his jacket pocket and pulling out a folded piece of paper, which he waved in front of Dominic. "We've sent for a special police vehicle to take you to San Luis. Tomorrow morning you'll face the magistrate, and it will be up to him to decide whether to hold you for trial. Meanwhile, you may consider yourself under arrest."

Chapter 16

In no time the whole village was buzzing with the news of Dominic's arrest. It was all the ranch employees could talk about, and even the field workers were discussing it. Ricardo was surprised by the turn of events, but he kept his thoughts to himself. As he supervised the unloading of sacks of fertilizer from the ranch truck, he listened to the nonstop chatter of the crew and soon realized that only the investigators believed Dominic was guilty.

"It's a frame-up," one man said.

"Those two officers are idiots!" another exclaimed.

And a third declared, "But he's in trouble anyway, if he can't prove his innocence."

Ricardo called them angrily to order. "That's enough. Let's get this truck unloaded."

When Inspector Otijo informed Eviana and Lee that Dominic was in custody, both women went pale with shock. "Dominic Fontanera is innocent!" Lee cried. "You're making a terrible mistake!"

Eviana's first impulse was to back up her sister-in-law, but then she recalled Dominic's reactions when she'd first told them about her suspicions. Hadn't he reproached her for informing the authorities?

Lee turned toward her. "Please, Eviana, tell the inspector that it's crazy to accuse Dominic."

That put an end to her hesitations. Dominic's influence had always loomed very large in her life, and she had always believed in his loyalty and integrity. "I'm convinced of his innocence!" she declared vehemently. "Besides, he had no reason to want to kill my brother."

"We'll just have to see about that," Otijo murmured noncommittally. As he turned to go Lee impulsively followed him.

"Inspector, may I see Dominic?"

Slowly he nodded. "For a short while, if you like. I'll go with you."

Dominic was staring bleakly out of his window when the door opened and Lee walked in. At once he was on his feet. Then he noticed Otijo standing behind her.

Lee smiled encouragingly. "I just wanted to tell you that we all know you're innocent, Dominic. Even Eviana."

"I wish I could say the same for him," he replied glumly, looking over her shoulder.

Lee realized that the officer had followed her into the room. "Inspector," she pleaded, "couldn't I have a minute alone with *Señor* Fontanera?"

When Otijo seemed to hesitate, Dominic said wryly, "It's all right, inspector. I won't bite her."

"I suppose...." Otijo conceded, smiling faintly. "But just for a few minutes." Quietly he left, closing the door behind him.

"Dominic," Lee blurted out, wringing her hands, "I can't imagine how this happened, and I'm certain Eviana never intended...Dominic?"

He was slowly moving closer to her with an enigmatic expression on his face. It was the same emotion she had glimpsed in his eyes once before, when she had extended a gesture of tenderness to him and he had recoiled with an apology for "taking liberties." *Damn this Argentinian class system*! she thought.

When he was very close, he took her hands in his and pressed them to his lips. "There's so much circumstancial evidence against me," he told her raggedly. "And they refuse to listen to logic. I'm afraid all your good wishes won't help me. They've built quite a case, Lee."

"No," she breathed, shaking her head stubbornly. "They can't convict you. I won't let them." Her throat constricted painfully.

And just as suddenly, he was holding her in his arms, in a gentle, protective embrace such as she'd never received from Fernando, even during the first delirious weeks of their marriage. Lee wept with the irony of it. Dominic was comforting *her*, when he was the one who stood to be imprisoned—or worse—if found guilty. "Oh, Dominic..." she moaned softly. "I'm so sorry." She clung tightly to him, feeling the warmth of his breath on her neck, the strength of his arms pressing into her back, and wishing...wishing.... If only, to protect himself, he would say something, do something...!

There was a muted click behind her and Inspector Otijo was standing in the doorway, clearing his throat. Reluctantly, Lee let go of Dominic. "Be brave," he whispered as she stepped away. Numbly, she turned and followed the officer out the door.

THE VEHICLE ORDERED by the two investigators arrived late in the afternoon and pulled up alongside the bungalow. Eviana and Lee watched from a distance as the rear doors of the van were flung open. Many of the *peons* and their families had gathered at the main gate of the house to watch the officers take Dominic away. Even Dr. Chandler, notified by the event by one of his patients, had rushed over to bolster his friend's spirits.

As Dominic emerged, blinking, into the bright afternoon sun, the crowd began to call encouragement to him. The two investigators, worried about the possible eruption of trouble, hurried him toward the van. Just as he was about to step into it, however, a woman suddenly broke away from the knot of spectators and ran forward with a shrill cry.

"No!" She collapsed in sobs at the feet of the police officers. Raising a face streaming with tears, she panted, "He didn't do it! It was me! I did it!"

Otijo shot a knowing look toward his young partner.

"Samantha!" Dominic cried. "Do you know what you're saying?"

"The truth! I can't live with it any longer!" she said in a strangled voice.

A commotion near the stables distracted the attention of some of the crowd from the drama in the back of the van. Julian Cartes had crumpled to the ground. As Dr. Chandler hurried over to him,

Otijo and Garcia herded both Dominic and Samantha back inside the bungalow.

"Now, what's this all about?" Otijo demanded in
a gruff voice as he closed the door behind them.

Samantha sank down on the edge of the bed, her
eyes still bright with tears as she explained in a
tremulous voice, "I swear I never meant to kill
Fernando. I loved him! But something strange
seemed to be coming over him. He began avoiding
me, and I got scared. I thought he might drop me
after learning that his wife was pregnant. The fear
was driving me crazy. Then one morning, after
waiting for him in vain, I went out to meet him on
the path, hoping to demand an explanation. Well,
when I found him, he told me that he still loved me,
but that he needed time to think things over. I
exploded with anger and we had a violent argument. Finally I couldn't take his insults anymore...." Overcome by the memory, she hung her
head and wept silently.

Inspector Otijo prompted her gently, "What happened then?"

"I grabbed the riding crop out of his hand and
reaching up as far as I could, I struck him across the
face with it. He cried out and clapped both hands to
his eyes. I saw blood on his forehead, and—and
then I panicked. I didn't know what I was doing.
There was an old shovel lying at the edge of the
field. I snatched it up and gave Carioca a whack
with it, and the horse took off. But Fernando
wasn't holding onto the reins...he lost his balance
and fell. One of his boots caught in the stir-
rup...oh, God! I ran along the trail after him and I
watched the workers stop the horse and free Fer-

nando. I was so scared—I knew I'd killed him. Anyway, I went back and wiped off the riding crop and the shovel so there wouldn't be any fingerprints. Then I hid the shovel and raced home before anyone even knew I'd been gone."

Tearfully she gazed into Otijo's round face. "When I heard that Dominic Fontanera had been arrested I didn't want him to pay for what I'd done. He's the only man I ever met who didn't use me or treat me with scorn," she concluded wretchedly. Then, lowering her face into her hands, she sobbed, "I never wanted to kill him, I never wanted to...."

As Garcia led Samantha outside to the van, Otijo turned to Dominic. "It appears that we made a mistake," he said simply. "Will you accept our apologies, *señor?*"

Dominic gazed into the inspector's face for a long moment before shaking his proffered hand.

ON JUNE 11 LEE GAVE BIRTH to a bouncing baby boy whom, to Eviana's delight, she decided to name Ramon, after Fernando's father. Eviana doted on the baby from the first moment, helping Rosa to give him his first bath and wrap him in the fine cotton blankets that had been waiting for him.

Exhausted but delighted, Lee was able to hand over her son to these two loving nannies with utter confidence. It took her a long while to get her strength back. Little Ramon, on the other hand, had emerged into the world with lusty kicks and cries. Eviana searched his tiny face for resemblances to the Valera family, but all he had inherited from his father had been dark eyes and golden skin.

His facial features, like his mother's, were delicate.

During her prolonged convalescence, Lee had time to think about the future, and she had to admit to herself that she no longer wanted to leave the Casa Rosada. Both her tormentors were gone—Fernando to his final reward and Samantha to a women's prison in San Luis, leaving Lee free to enjoy the way of life on the ranch to which she had grown accustomed. She loved Casa Rosada...but she had also loved Paris and Boston, and she had left them both without any qualms. No, there was something else keeping her here, an attachment that had taken root in her heart during one of the most vulnerable periods in her life, and for that reason alone she was still half-afraid to trust it.

She remembered standing on the front porch with Eviana, her vision clouding with tears, as she had stared in anguish at the two police officers escorting Dominic out of his bungalow. He had turned, his eyes searching, and Lee had shivered with a sudden chill. She hadn't felt half as bereaved at Fernando's graveside....

Dominic! she had thought. She owed him so much...and she wanted him so badly—wanted him to stay, wanted the chance to bring down his wall of reserve and to share the almost overpowering feeling that had swept over her, mingled with her dry-mouthed dread. Not until that second had she wanted to call it by its name—love, hopelessly involving, totally giving. But Dominic was stepping into the van, and it was too late. She didn't dare call out, either, for this Argentinian society was so class-conscious that she would probably only have embarrassed him....

So Lee had stood on the porch trembling, until Eviana mistook her reaction and offered to go inside and get her a shawl. Then Samantha had suddenly confessed, and what a welter of mixed feelings had assailed Lee at that moment: unutterable relief that Dominic was free coupled with the deep irrational fear that by making the ultimate sacrifice for him, Samantha had captured Dominic's gratitude, or worse still, his love.

THAT HAD BEEN BEFORE her son had been born. Now the time had come to make a decision—to go or to stay. And she was certainly free to choose. She knew Eviana's preference in the matter of course. But by staying, wouldn't she be letting herself in for new disappointments? What exactly had she read in Dominic's eyes that turbulent afternoon? Shouldn't she run from an emotion that might end in more heartbreak? For she had no proof that Dominic felt anything for her beyond friendship. Not for a moment during the past weeks had he departed from his usual friendly manner.

It wasn't Dominic who helped her decide, however, it was Eviana. One morning, while the two women were bending over little Ramon's cradle together, Eviana said tenderly, "Isn't he just adorable? Look at his little ears."

Lee remarked with a smile, "You've been a perfect nanny for him. But now that I'm back on my feet I can take over from you."

"Oh, not completely?" Eviana said anxiously. "He's such a joy to me right now. Please don't deprive me of him."

"Of course not, Eviana! But you mustn't grow too attached to Ramon," Lee advised her gently. "If we were to leave Argentina—"

"You're not leaving?" Eviana cried in alarm.

"I don't know.... I have to think about it...."

"There's no reason for you to go. This house belongs to you and your son. I know I haven't always been the friend you would have liked, but I've changed. We can live happily together here. I beg you, Lee, don't take Ramon away from Casa Rosada!"

Touched, Lee smiled at her. "You plead very persuasively. Perhaps Ramon will grow up on the ranch after all."

Later that day Lee went to join Dominic out at the corrals. He had just concluded the sale of a third of their horses to a ranch in the south pampas. The sale, which had included Carioca and Tampico, had had Eviana's wholehearted approval.

"Did you know that Eviana has asked me to stay on here at the ranch?" Lee said, watching his reactions carefully.

He gazed worriedly at her. "You've agreed to stay, haven't you?"

"Not yet. I'm still deciding."

"There's no decision to make. Your place is here," he stated.

"Are you sure of that?" She had to fight to keep her voice level.

"I'm positive." Suddenly his expression shifted. He was about to say something when Julian Cartes came over and cut him off.

"I'll have made my decision by this evening," Lee told him before leaving the corral.

That day Eviana announced the news at dinner: "I've convinced Lee not to leave Casa Rosada," she said happily. "She's decided to stay with us."

Looking around the table, Lee saw the same glow of relief and satisfaction in both foremen's eyes.

WINTER CAME. It was quite mild, making little change in the easy rhythm of life on the ranch. Little Ramon was awakening more and more to the wonders of the world that surrounded him. Eviana spent most of her time playing with her nephew, leaving Dominic and Ricardo to take care of the ranch and Lee to oversee them. Lee was discovering how challenging it could be to manage a large piece of property. This was the antidote she needed to the life of leisure that had made her so restless before. In fact, it was making a new woman of her. It also meant that she spent a great deal more time with Dominic and Ricardo, and she found that spending time with Dominic was in itself a powerful stimulant.

From time to time she would look up and find Ricardo staring intently at her, but once their eyes met and she had smiled at him his expression relaxed. It was rather disturbing, but Lee didn't let it bother her. They had all been through a trying summer. Besides, Ricardo, she realized was probably unused to the North American aggressiveness that Lee brought to her dealings with other ranchers and grain agents—unused to seeing it in a woman, at any rate. He'd get over it, she told herself.

Keeping a promise to herself, Lee was also learning to ride a horse, thanks to Dominic. She was a gifted student, and they were already able to undertake rambles through the fields from which she invariably returned with rosy cheeks and a ravenous appetite.

Lee's life would have been perfect, in fact, if only Dominic weren't holding her at arm's length. Her every attempt at familiarity, even when they were out riding together, miles from curious eyes and ears, was met with cool reserve. A certain amount of closeness was natural and could be expected between a riding instructor and his student, if this student weren't also his employer, his manner seemed to be telling her. And the camaraderie that might customarily mark the relationship between a trusted employee and his employer was also not permissible, because she was a woman. Lee found herself growing more frustrated daily. Every fiber of her being recalled the tenderness of his embrace, the thrill of his touch, and she wanted it again, forever. She loved him passionately. Couldn't he see how she felt? Was he totally deaf and blind to the signals her heart kept sending him, the longing looks, the tentative smiles, the repeated attempts to reestablish a relationship based on affection as well as on respect?

Or was he giving her her answer? Was his very aloofness a tacit rejection? Was it Lee who was deliberately ignoring a clearly sent message? She thought she would go mad wondering about Dominic's feelings. She felt like a teenager, agonizing over a crush and fighting the premonition that what she and Dominic had would turn out to be totally unfounded.

One day just before dinnertime, as Rosa and

Luisa were taking some hot soup out to the stable hands and Eviana was putting little Ramon to bed in another wing of the house, Lee was arranging dried flowers in a vase in the living room. Suddenly she became aware of a presence behind her. She whirled around and found herself face to face with Ricardo.

"You frightened me," she reproached him smilingly. Then she noticed his eyes, which were gleaming strangely.

"I had to see you alone," he murmured.

Suddenly uneasy, she managed to keep her voice impersonal as she asked, "What about?"

"What about?" he repeated with a laugh. His breath reeked of alcohol.

"Ricardo, you've been drinking!" she exclaimed.

"Only enough to give me courage. I had to tell you that I love you," he declared, uttering the confession in a single gasp. Unexpectedly he lunged forward and caught her roughly around the waist.

"Let me go! Have you lost your mind?" she cried, struggling to get free.

"Yes, I have. I'm crazy about you! I've been waiting for months to tell you this. How I've dreamed of holding you in my arms...." And he tightened his embrace, squeezing her against his powerful chest until she grew too faint to fight him any more.

"Every day I lived for a look or a smile from you," he rambled on drunkenly. "I've loved you from the moment I first saw you in the airport waiting room in San Luis, with your blond hair and your lovely face. I had never before envied Fernando Valera for his money or his position, but from that day onward I envied him for his wife. Well, he's gone now.

I'm here and I love you, and we have the right to live...."

Gathering her strength to resist him, she protested, "Let me go or I'll call for help!"

"Nobody will come. I waited for the perfect moment, my darling. Nobody can hear you. You and I can go far away from here, make a brand new life for ourselves."

"How dare you?" Lee could hear the note of panic in her voice.

He tried to kiss her but she twisted her head from one side to the other, evading his searching lips. Finally, angered, he seized her wrists in a grip so tight that she cried out.

"I'm not good enough for you, is that it? You'd rather have the Valera fortune! Yet you never put on these airs with Dominic! Don't you think I've noticed how you look at him, how you flirt with him? I threw Eviana aside for you! I—"

The sequence of events that followed happened so quickly that Lee almost missed it. All at once Dominic was there, spinning Ricardo around and hitting him with a right cross that sent him flying across the room. When Ricardo had recovered from the blow, Lee was still cowering defensively against the wall and Dominic was standing protectively beside her, ready to fend off anymore unwanted advances. Eviana was standing in the doorway, with an expression of utter disgust on her face.

"Get out of here!" she commanded in an icy voice. "Tomorrow morning you'll turn your books over to Dominic and leave this ranch with three months' severance pay. I never want to see you again."

The announcement sobered Ricardo immediately. He got to his feet, staggered out the door and disappeared down the corridor.

As soon as he was gone, Lee began to stammer, "I...couldn't reason with him...he was out of his mind."

"God only knows what's been going through it the past couple of hours anyway, besides whiskey fumes," Dominic muttered.

"Eviana, you were very hard on him," Lee said. "It was the alcohol that made him behave that way."

But Eviana shook her head, her expression neutral. "He had to go," she replied. "There was no other way. I'll have to tell Rosa not to set a place at dinner for him, so if you'll excuse me...."

Alone together, Lee and Dominic exchanged troubled glances.

"I'm glad I happened to come to dinner so early," he said at last, in a stiff voice. "It enabled me to protect your honor, *señora*."

Lee felt torn in two. Half of her wanted to collapse in tears and the other half wanted to explode. "Don't call me that," she said shortly. "And if all you were doing was defending my honor, then I must be blind as well as insensitive."

"What?"

"You didn't see the look on your face as you watched Ricardo get up off the floor. You looked ready to kill him, Dominic!" She moved so that she was standing right in front of him. "You do have feelings for me, don't you?" she asked softly.

"I guess it's no use trying to hide it any longer," he sighed a little sheepishly. "Otijo and Garcia knew how I felt about you. They figured that that was my motive for killing Fernando. And somebody must have told them, which means that somebody must have realized what my feelings were toward you. I didn't mean to hit Ricardo that hard, but when I saw you struggling in his arms something inside me snapped—" He gestured vaguely.

Lee couldn't hold herself back any longer. "Why didn't you say something? Wasn't it obvious how I felt about *you*?"

"I kept quiet because I knew it was impossible for us, in spite of how we felt. You're a Valera and I'm just—"

"I'm a Carlisle," she corrected him firmly, "as long as we're stating genealogies. I *married* a Valera. There's a difference."

"Not in Argentina," Dominic shook his head.

"But who's going to object?" she protested. "Eviana? She fell in love with Ricardo, remember? If a real Valera could do it, then so can I."

"She could no more have married Ricardo than I could marry you," he stated flatly.

"Do you want to marry me?" Lee asked, pouncing on what had probably been a slip of the tongue.

"It doesn't matter what I want," he explained with infuriating patience. "The class barriers in this country are very strict."

"Dominic, I was wrong before," she said abruptly. "All right—I'm a Valera. What does that make me? Rich?" He nodded. "Powerful?" He nodded again. "Powerful enough to break a taboo and set a social precedent if I feel like it?"

"*Señora*," he began guardedly.

"I told you not to call me that. Dominic, I love you. Do you love me?" There were tears of frustration in her voice.

Taking a deep breath, he replied, "Yes, I do. But that doesn't alter the fact that I'm just—"

"You're the man I love and want to marry," she said fervently. "I don't care what you do for a living, don't you see? If I had come back from Europe as Fernando's secretary instead of as his wife, you and I would already be married. Instead there are all these stupid traditions keeping us apart—it makes no sense!" Lee sank down onto the divan and buried her face in her hands. She could feel the tears wash down her cheeks, but let them flow unstemmed.

Suddenly Dominic was beside her, his strong arms forming a protective circle around her as she leaned sobbing against his chest. When the worst of her emotional storm had passed, they were still sitting together on the divan, wrapped in each other's arms.

"Lee," he murmured uncertainly in her ear. "Do you really think we have a chance?"

Her heart began racing with joy as she gazed hungrily into his face. "Oh, yes!" she breathed. "Oh, yes, Dominic!"

"I love you, Lee," he said simply. At last the mask had dropped. Lee saw before her a whole man, warm and loving and throbbing with passion. Slowly he lowered his lips onto hers, making the blood rush through her veins as they shared a deep, binding promise of tenderness. The future would be theirs.